MR. JUNE

HEROES OF ROGUE VALLEY: CALENDAR GUYS
BOOK 6

ANN ROTH

OLIVERHEBERBOOKS

Published by Oliver-Heber Books

0 9 8 7 6 5 4 3 2 1

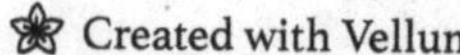 Created with Vellum

INTRODUCTION

Welcome to Ann Roth's exciting new series, Heroes of Rogue Valley: Calendar Guys series. Twelve months, 12 gorgeous firefighter heroes and the women who steal into their hearts and forever change their lives.

Meet Mr. June:

Firefighter Max Meier avoids serious relationships at all costs. That way no one gets hurt. Max has caused more than enough pain in his life, including blaming himself for his baby sister's death years ago. Teacher Megan Spenser is no stranger to loss and heartache, but unlike Max she still believes in love. Megan's warmth chips away at the protective shield around Max's heart and threatens to lay him bare. Can he overcome the past that has forever scarred him and take a chance on love?

Mr. June—Max Meier
    Age 34, 6'1", 188 pounds of muscle
    Single
    Proud Senior Firefighter
    Time with Guff's Lake Fire Department: 13
years

1

The final day of Career Day week had never been like this.

In Megan Spenser's ten years as a third-grade elementary-education teacher at Guff's Lake School, she'd met accountants, doctors, dentists, insurance agents, police officers, and a host of other professionals.

But until today she'd never met a firefighter, let alone a local celebrity of sorts. Max Meier, aka Mr. June on the fire department calendar, here in her classroom!

Proceeds from sales of the calendar went to the benefit fund, established to help victims of fires. Such a good cause, and with a different attractive male featured each month, no woman in town could resist owning a copy.

In person, Max was even more striking. With his impressive size, muscled body, and chiseled face—yes, he had the requisite lean cheeks, classic Greek nose, and strong jaw— Wow. Just wow.

Dreamy looks aside, the biggest tug at Megan's heartstrings came from the way the big man clasped the little hand of his niece, Ava Josephs, a towhead cutie in Megan's class.

Megan was aware that the girl's father had died when she was a toddler and that her uncle was a firefighter, but she hadn't known his name.

As the children and a parent or stand-in entered the classroom, Megan offered each guest a smile and handshake. No reason not to greet Max the same way. Even if she did tremble a little inside.

She extended her arm. "I'm Miss Spenser— Megan."

Dressed in turnout gear, aka his firefighter uniform, yet another cause for heart palpitations, Max passed his helmet to his niece. "Max Meier."

His warm hand dwarfed Megan's. His eyes, an unusual whiskey brown, flitted over her before he released his grasp.

She suffered a moment of acute fandom. Wait till Ingrid heard about this. Then again, her best friend, who taught fourth grade across the hall, had likely already noticed him.

As flummoxed as Megan felt, she wasn't about to do anything silly like fawn over him or blush. Why was she thinking about that here in the classroom?

She turned to Ava. "Please take your seat, and

Max, you'll sit with today's other guests." Megan gestured at the eight folding chairs in front of the giant map of the world against the wall. "I see a place next to Cody's dad."

"Max isn't my daddy, he's my uncle," Ava reminded her.

For a split second Megan's gaze collided with the firefighter's. Losing her father at such a young age had to have affected the little girl. Megan had certainly been traumatized when she'd lost hers. Although she'd been twelve, years older. A loss like that stayed with a person.

She nodded. "I remember. I'm very glad you brought him with you today."

The loving grin Max showered on Ava melted Megan. While he joined the other guests, his niece took her seat at the table she shared with three other boys and girls.

The bell rang, and Megan started the school day, taking attendance and setting the morning. "As you know, this is our last day of Career Day. Remember to be respectful."

She directed her next comments to the adults. "Because there are eight of you and we have limited time, I'll be using a five-minute timer so that everyone has a chance to speak. When you finish, the students will have five minutes to ask questions. Halfway through, we'll break for recess.

"We'll finish shortly after lunch. Those who can't stay will go first. If you have the time and would like to join us for the meal, you're welcome, but I need to let the cafeteria know. How many of you are planning to stay?"

A man and a woman raised their hands. After glancing at her uncle, Ava's brow furrowed and her hand shot up.

"Yes, Ava?" Megan asked.

"Is it okay if I ask Uncle Max something?" Megan nodded, and her student gave her uncle a wide-eyed look. "Will you eat with me?"

Max scratched his neck. "I wasn't planning to."

"Please, Uncle Max? Can't you work on the cabinet later?"

Everyone looked confused at that.

"When I'm off-duty, I make custom furniture," Max explained.

Interesting. Megan raised her eyebrow. "Will you be talking about that today?"

"Not enough time. Sure it's okay if I stick around for lunch?"

"Yes."

"Then yeah, I'll eat with you, Ava." He shrugged and smiled at his niece.

Oh, to be the beneficiary of that gorgeous grin. Megan's heart did a cartwheel in her chest. "We'll start with those who aren't able to stay. Cody, please come to the front of the room and introduce your father."

～

As SPEAKERS TALKED about their jobs and answered questions, Max's mind wandered. He hadn't intended to stay for lunch, but he never had been able to resist his niece.

He wouldn't mind getting to know her teacher, either. Early thirties, golden shoulder-length hair anchored back with clips, and a great mouth...

Ava chattered nonstop about Megan Spenser, but Max had never imagined she was such a looker. He could do without the modest, knee-length dress and tights, but her calves and ankles were slender and shapely. A leg man, he appreciated that.

Was she single? Couldn't hurt to find out.

He wasn't seeing anyone right now. Didn't want a girlfriend—he didn't do serious—but he enjoyed dating.

By the time the recess bell rang, the kids were antsy to get up and move. The guests who had already spoken had left.

"It's time for recess," Megan said. "Class, please get your coats, then line up against the wall. For those guests still here, we'll be back in approximately twenty minutes. Take this time to relax."

The kids stood and in an orderly fashion filed out of the room to their lockers. Max was impressed. Megan had a solid hold on the kids and they seemed eager to obey. Like Ava, they appeared to like their teacher a lot.

After recess Career Day continued, with adults leaving as they finished. By lunch all but Max and the two others who had opted in for lunch remained to speak. Ready to eat, he accompanied his niece to the cafeteria.

To his disappointment, Megan had disappeared. Too bad—he wanted to talk to her and get to know more about her.

One of the lunch attendants gave him a folding chair to sit on, and a good thing. He wouldn't have fit on the bench at the table. Hunched over his plate, he ate the same standard school fare, which was so-so and not nearly enough to fill his empty belly. Several adults policed the cafeteria, making sure there were no food fights or other disruptions.

A second recess followed lunch, then back to class to finish up Career Day. Max was last up. Everyone seemed interested, including Megan. She sat forward in her seat at the desk with a rapt expression on her face. He liked that.

With only five minutes to speak, he stuck with a few basics. "Any questions?" he asked when he finished.

Half a dozen kids raised their hands. A boy bouncing in his seat went first. "How come you call your uniform 'turnout clothes'?"

"Great question," Max said. "First, this is more than a uniform. These clothes are made of special material that protects us from heat and flames. The name comes from our practice of 'turning out' our pants over the tops of our boots, which allows us to step directly into the boots and pull the pants and suspenders up in one move. That saves time, and when we're called to a fire, getting there fast can mean the difference between success and failure. We aim for success —keeping people safe and saving buildings."

He fielded several more questions before Megan signaled "time out" and joined him up front. She wasn't tall, about level with his Adam's apple.

"Thank you, Mr. Meier. Class, let's show our appreciation." She led the applause with a whole lot of enthusiasm. "Please pull out your books and read while I speak with Mr. Meier outside," she instructed when the kids settled down.

She and Max stepped into the hall. "You made a big hit. The entire class hung onto your every word."

From what he'd observed, so had she. "They were an easy group to please." Her eyes were a startling blue green. And that mouth... The plump bottom lip snagged his attention and held it.

Megan touched her lips. "Do I have something on my mouth?"

Realizing he was staring, he jerked his gaze up. "No. What did you want to talk about? Is Ava doing okay? Her mom hasn't said anything."

"Your niece is wonderful. Here's what I'm thinking—my students would really benefit from a full class about safety. Do you think you could come again?"

Max didn't see why not. "Sure. I'll need an okay from Captain Comings. I'll talk to him Monday."

"Thanks. I'm still blown away by the two, back-to-back, twenty-four shifts you work each week—with limited sleep during that time."

He shrugged. "After thirteen years, I'm used to it."

"And I thought teaching was exhausting. Do you think you can come back before the end of the month? Thursdays or Fridays work best for us."

With only two weeks left in January, that didn't leave much time. "That shouldn't be a problem. Here's my card. If you'll give me your email address and phone number, I'll get back to you so we can coordinate."

Megan supplied the information, and he added it to his address book. He liked her and appreciated having her contact info.

She glanced at the closed door. "My students are waiting. Thanks again. It's obvious Ava is very proud of you."

Max wasn't good with compliments, but knowing his niece was proud of him felt good. As did having her teacher's contact info.

Ready to eat again, he exited the school lot and drove to the nearest fast-food place.

2

As always on Friday afternoon, after the students left the building, the school's twenty-five teachers stayed behind to straighten up their classrooms and talk among themselves.

Today, Seretha Herman, the principal, had called a brief Friday afternoon meeting in the teachers lounge. Megan, Ingrid, and several of their peers arrived early. While they waited for Seretha and the others, they chatted about the day.

"Max—whew, what a hottie," Ingrid murmured.

Every female, young and old, in the room agreed. The men didn't argue. How could they, when it was true?

He also seemed like a great guy. He'd left Megan's classroom hours ago, but she was still thinking about him. His obvious enthusiasm for his career, his engaging smile and rapport with her students, his willingness to come back on one of his days off.

"Mr. April, the firefighter who conducted the district-wide fire and safety assembly a few weeks before the school year started, was every bit as delicious," Ingrid added.

Megan shook her head. "And to think I was out with food poisoning that day."

The rest of the teachers wandered in, followed by Seretha, and the conversation ended.

"I won't keep you long," the principal promised. "I wanted to let you know that Bobby 'Football' Smith's all-school, anti-bullying assembly scheduled for next month has been postponed until March. We need something else for February, and I'm looking for suggestions."

Of the three elementary schools in town, Guff's Lake School was the only one with grades kindergarten through eight housed in one building.

"At this late date?" one of the sixth-grade teachers said. "That's only three weeks away."

People threw out ideas but nothing that seemed interesting. Seretha narrowed her eyes in thought. "Tell me about the firefighter who came to your class today, Megan. Did your students like him?"

Megan nodded. "Max did a great job. The entire class was mesmerized." She'd been equally enthralled. "He and I discussed his coming back soon for a safety lesson."

"Could you persuade him to offer an expanded lesson for the entire school instead?" Seretha asked.

Most of the teachers liked the idea.

"I have no idea what his schedule is, but I'll certainly ask," Megan said.

"Keep us posted. All right, everyone, we're done. Have a great weekend."

Ingrid and Megan strolled toward their respective classrooms to collect their things and go home.

"Lucky you—you get to call Max." Ingrid sighed. "If you're too busy, I'm happy to step in."

"Ha ha. He's expecting my call."

"You don't seem excited about that. Maybe you need glasses. This isn't just any old firefighter. We're talking about Max Meier."

"Believe me, I've noticed," Megan said. "He probably has women falling all over him. I refuse to be one of them."

"That wouldn't stop me."

"I'm not you. If he's interested, let him do the chasing."

"Because you don't want to seem desperate and needy."

"Which I'm not." Megan had never considered herself remotely like that until Matt, the then-love of her life, had dumped her the night of the high school junior prom. He'd accused her of being both desperate and needy, claiming she tried way too hard to please and hold onto him.

Looking back later, she'd understood what he meant. She'd been lonely, mainly because her mother had recently married Bennett. Megan had disapproved. Anything else felt like a betrayal to her father. Even if he had been gone five years, replacing him with another man seemed wrong. She'd also felt left out, which was why she'd turned to Matt.

The breakup with him had changed everything. Crushed, she'd turned to her mother and by default, Bennett. With their love and assurances, she'd made peace with the marriage. She'd also moved on and put her heartbreak behind her.

Until last year, when Tyler had broken up with her. Eerily, he'd cited the same reasons Matt had. When she'd been sure they were a forever couple.

"But I am beginning to wonder and all right, getting a little anxious," she admitted. At almost thirty-three, her best child-bearing years would soon be behind her. "Is it so far-fetched to want a family of my own? Why do most men today seem to want to extend their adolescence as long as they can?"

"If I had the answers to that... You don't need a husband to have a baby."

Not long ago Megan's mom and Bennett had voiced the same sentiment. "I do if I want my child's daddy in the picture."

Having lost her father on the cusp of puberty,

Megan knew the importance of a male role model. She was determined to have a family of her own. "Meet you here in five."

Returning to the classroom, Megan shrugged into her coat and grabbed her purse and papers she needed to grade over the weekend. As usual, she and Ingrid walked to the parking lot together. As they exited the building, a brisk wind gusted.

"Brr," Ingrid said, wrapping a wool scarf around her neck.

Megan put on her gloves. "Several more months of this cold—ugh." The conversation returned to men. "There are plenty of fish in the sea, and one of them is searching for me," she said, repeating the cliché her mom had comforted her with since Matt.

"Okay, but if for some reason you and that one fish don't meet up, then what?"

"Spoilsport," Megan muttered, although her friend had a point.

At one time, certain of her mother's wisdom in matters of love, Megan had truly believed her forever guy was searching for her and that eventually, he would find her.

Now, with time marching on and a whole lot of heartache under her belt... She'd become jaded. Maybe it was time to switch to plan B.

"I swore I'd never try online dating again, but without a date in sight...I guess I should." She mimed sticking a finger down her throat.

"You never know," Ingrid said. "I've met some

decent guys through In the Cards. No one I flipped out over, but not half bad."

She meant James, the man she was currently seeing. "Are you and James getting together later?"

Ingrid shook her head. "I haven't heard from him in over a week."

"Aw, I'm sorry."

"I'm not. He's not bad, but kissing him was like kissing a good friend—there was no spark. Besides, I'm too tired to spend the evening with anyone. I'll be lucky to stay awake until ten."

"Friday nights are like that."

Then and there, Megan made up her mind. "I may as well join In the Cards. I'll give it six months. What are you doing tomorrow night?"

"No plans yet. Hey, we should go out together. It's been ages since we went to Lucky Joe's. Guess who's playing there Saturday? Mello—that local group we've been hearing so much about. They're supposed to be awesome, and this is our chance to find out."

A Saturday night at Lucky Joe's guaranteed a lively crowd and plenty of dance partners, especially with a hot Guff's Lake band. "I'm in," Megan said.

"If we go early, we'll be able to get a good table and have dinner before the dancing starts. Who knows—we could both meet our Mr. Rights."

"Wouldn't that be nice." But doubtful. So far,

most of the men Megan had met at the dance bar seemed to be out for a good time, period. "I'd offer to drive, but the last few days, my car has been giving me problems. Sometimes it doesn't want to start."

"You don't need that kind of trouble, especially in the middle of winter. Get your mechanic to take a look."

"I will. Saturdays at Al's Auto Repair are usually booked, but maybe he can squeeze me in. All I have to do is remember to call. Which I'll do as soon as I get in the car."

"If he can schedule you, let me know and I'll give you a ride home. Anyway, it's my turn to drive Saturday night."

Standing between their cars, they finalized plans for dinner and dancing, then parted company.

To Megan's relief, her car started right up. Al didn't pick up, but she left a message. On the drive home, she thought about Saturday night. Who knew, Ingrid could be right and they'd both meet guys they liked.

If not... That's what the online dating site was for.

~

IN THE NEONATAL section of Rogue Valley General Hospital, Megan rained a loving smile on the fussing newborn in her arms. Her job was to provide comfort and help calm him so that he could take a bottle and sleep.

The tiny boy, as yet unnamed, had been born to a crack-addicted mother, and like most infants in his situation was distressed and uncomfortable. Hence the equipment and monitors along the wall of the room, which otherwise was as cozy as any nursery.

Poor little guy had a rough road ahead. Megan's heart ached for him, as it did for all the babies she'd rocked in her two years as a volunteer. She prayed his mother got straight. If not, she hoped he found a loving home.

As a novice volunteer she'd considered fostering one of the babies. After careful thought, she'd ruled it out. A baby in this condition would need intensive, round-the-clock TLC for the foreseeable future, and she wasn't up to the task. But during the two hours she was here she gave her all.

"It's going be okay," she soothed.

Her soft tone and the gentle to and fro of the rocking chair soon quieted him. Filled with tenderness, she brushed her lips across his dark brown hair.

She cuddled him until Sue, one of the weekend nurses, came in to relieve her.

Sue smiled. "You did a really good job with him. But then, you usually do."

"I enjoy it. Oddly enough, rocking and soothing him gives me peace and calm."

"He senses that. See how well he's sleeping?"

After checking to ensure he was swaddled properly, Megan carefully placed him in his crib. "I'll see you next week," she promised.

If he was still here. That depended on how quickly his tiny body rid itself of the drugs.

Walking away made her sad, but at least she and Ingrid had something fun planned for tonight. Eager to go out and dance away the melancholy, Megan went home to change clothes and get ready.

3

Saturday night Max met up with Tony, Ethan, and Nate for pizza and beer at Harvey's, the best pizza joint in town. As always, the eatery was packed.

"How did the thing at Ava's school go yesterday?" Tony asked over the noise as they chowed down.

"There wasn't enough time to do a thorough job, but otherwise it wasn't half bad. The teacher invited me back to do a safety workshop for the class. All I need is the captain's go-ahead."

Tony frowned. "On one of your days off?" When Max nodded he said, "That's dedication."

"Hey, if the kids learn something..." Plus, Max would get to see Megan again. He was definitely interested.

"They will. Speaking of training, what have you got lined up for us the rest of the month?"

A few weeks ago Captain Comings had put Max in charge of selecting sessions for this year's in-house training. Max intended to do a bang-up job.

The payoff? A recommendation from the captain, which Max needed in order to secure a part-time gig teaching fire safety at the Guff's Lake branch of Rogue Valley Community College.

With most of the pizza gone, Ethan checked his watch. "I need to get going."

He played sax with Mello, a dynamite jazz fusion/rock band performing tonight at Lucky Joe's. Max, Tony, and Nate intended to head over there shortly, to enjoy the good music and a night of dancing with hot women.

Some forty minutes later, arriving at Lucky Joe's in separate cars—a guy never knew when he might want to go home with someone—Max again met up with his two crewmates.

Mello hadn't started yet, but the place was hopping with locals and others from around Rogue Valley. Everyone was eager to hear the area's top local band.

Ethan had placed a "reserved" sign on a table near the wall—a great place to people watch. As soon as Max and his buds sat down, they snagged a waitress and ordered a pitcher and snacks.

"Lots of fine ladies here tonight," Tony said. "Don't look now, Max, but at my ten o'clock there are two hot women checking you out."

"Yeah?" Max glanced casually over his shoulder—and spotted Megan and another teacher from her school.

All of a sudden, the evening looked even better than he'd imagined.

Even from twenty feet away he could tell Megan was blushing. He grinned and waved. Megan returned a quick smile.

"You know her?" Tony asked.

"That's Megan Spenser—Ava's teacher."

"I'll bet every little boy in her class is in love with her. Makes me want to go back to elementary school and be her teacher's pet."

The manager of Lucky Joe's stepped onto the stage and introduced the six-person band as the musicians appeared from the back and took their places. Max and his buds hooted and whistled along with everyone else. The first song was loud and rhythmic—great for dancing.

"You gonna sit around sipping your beer all night, or ask her to dance?" Tony said. "'Cause if you don't, I will."

Max was already on his feet. "You dance with her friend."

Not bothering to wait for his bud, he made his way toward Megan.

~

MEGAN HAD JUST FINISHED the last of her dinner wine when the band struck up a song with a toe-tapping beat that made her want to dance. With or without a partner.

She noticed Max coming her way at the same

moment Ingrid elbowed her. "OMG, here come Max and one of his sexy firefighter friends."

Megan's heart skipped but she stayed cool. Let him pursue me.

"Hey," Max greeted her over the music.

"Hi."

"Hello there," Ingrid cooed.

Max nodded at her. "I know you from Guff's Lake School. You're Ingrid, right? Meet Tony."

Ingrid gave Max's handsome friend the flirty smile she was so good at. "I recognize you from the calendar."

"Mr. July at your service," Tony drawled, with a lazy, utterly charming smile.

Definitely attractive, but not as magnetic as Max.

Tony held out his hand to Ingrid. "Would you like to dance?"

"I'd love to." Ingrid rose and they headed for the dance floor.

"How about you?" Max asked.

Megan stood. "With this band it's impossible to sit still. They're fantastic."

"I'll pass that along to Ethan, the guy on sax. He's a crewmate of mine—Mr. September on the calendar."

"I knew he looked familiar."

"I come here a lot but this is the first time I've seen you," Max said, leaning in to speak into her ear.

His deep voice vibrated through her. He also

smelled yummy—spicy and sexy. Her insides quivered and she almost forgot about making him work to draw her interest. But not quite.

She stepped back. "If I'm lucky, I make it several times a year."

"I'm glad you're here." His eyes flared with heat.

He was? Ignoring the thrill rippling through her, Megan glanced away.

On the dance floor, he put his hand on the small of her back and guided her through the gyrating crowd. The possessive gesture further weakened her defenses.

Dancing women shot her envious looks. If she'd been one of them she'd have felt the same. And here she was, about to dance with the hottest guy in the room.

Between the loud music and the hustle and bustle on the dance floor, conversation was impossible. The music took over and she and Max did their thing. For a big man, he was light on his feet.

"You're good," she said when the song ended.

"Not half as good as you."

His appreciative gaze roved from her hair to her stacked leather-heel western boots, and she was glad she'd worn jeans and a top that flattered her.

"Do you mind if we talk shop?" she asked.

"You mean about my next visit to your classroom? Sure—tell me what you want."

She wanted to know what his arms felt like around her, and whether he kissed as good as he looked. Instead she blanked her expression. "Since yesterday, things have—"

The band started up again and Max cupped his ear. She shouted in order to be heard. "My principal wondered if instead of giving a safety lesson to just my class, you'd be open to an all-school assembly."

He squinted at her. "Can't hear you. It's too noisy to talk in here. Let's go someplace quieter."

Leery he'd make a pass at her—no, that she couldn't trust herself to rebuff him if he did—she glanced around. "Where?"

"On the other side of the building. Come on."

He grasped her arm. Her body, happy to feel a man in close proximity after a long drought, went giddy, and it was hard not to collapse at his feet in a pool of want. Avoiding the crush of dancers helped her focus, and she made off the dance floor and past the bar without a hitch.

Good work, she congratulated herself as the doors closed behind them. Now if she could just remember to play it cool...

4

The crowd outside the dance and bar area was sparse, but Max kept hold of Megan. In the space of one fast dance, his attraction for her had grown. Her cherry red blouse fluttering against to her breasts and hips would tempt a eunuch.

Max wanted to get up close and personal with her. Real close. But hell, they'd just met. Still, a guy could try.

He slid his palm up her back, testing for a reaction. She stiffened, gave him a dirty look, and pulled out of his grasp.

"What?" he said, holding both hands up.

"We came out here to talk."

No fooling around tonight. Message received loud and clear. "Do you have a boyfriend?" he asked.

"If I did, he'd be here with me."

Good to know. "I'm single, too," he said, and

wondered at her knowing nod. "I like your hair that way."

She touched her head. "What way?"

"Without clips. Wavy and free."

"You mean a curly mess. If I wore it like this when I taught, it'd just get in the way."

She tucked several offending locks behind her ears. Max resisted the urge to pull them free again. "Looks okay to me." He gestured ahead. "This way."

"You never said where we're going."

"Past the restrooms, around the corner, and down the hall. At the far end, there are places to sit."

"Really? I never even noticed the hallway."

"I only know about it because I did a safety inspection of the building last year." He nodded at the sofa and chairs ahead. "That's where I figured we'd sit, but it already looks crowded."

Two couples around his age had pulled the armchairs into a private grouping, leaving only the loveseat. When the women spotted him, they both straightened their spines.

"You're on the calendar," one said, with a starstruck smile. "Mr. June, right?"

If Max had a dime for every time someone recognized him... He nodded. "That's me. Mind if my lady friend and I sit here?"

"Not at all."

The couples resumed their conversation.

Megan sat at one end of the loveseat and

linked her hands together in her lap. Not wanting to crowd her and earn another dirty look, Max stuck to his end. Given the compact size of the thing only a few scant inches separated them.

"Everyone seems to know you from the calendar," Megan said. "Do you get tired of that?"

He glanced at the two women, then cupped his hand around the side of his mouth and lowered his voice. "Hell, yeah."

"You're a good sport about it."

"Hey, it's for a good cause."

"I contributed. The calendar is hanging in my kitchen." And like every woman she knew, she drooled over the gorgeous men.

"We appreciate that."

"You're the first firefighter I've met," she said. "I'm curious—aside from dealing with fires and doing inspections, what else do firefighters do?"

"A lot. We do workshops and conduct classes on CPR and other lifesaving medical techniques. The bulk of our emergency calls are medical, and everyone on the team takes a turn at a month-long paramedic rotation. It works out to about three times a year. I'm scheduled for next month."

"You're a certified paramedic?"

"That's right. No job applicant is seriously considered without a paramedic certification."

"Wow. You wear so many hats in your work. I had no idea."

"If I'd had time yesterday, I would have mentioned some of my responsibilities. I'll do that when I come back. You mentioned an assembly?"

She nodded. "For the whole school."

In his thirteen years as a firefighter, Max had done his share of all-school programs. "Sure, I'll put something together. How long should it last and when are you thinking?"

"Ninety minutes, the first Friday in February."

"That's only about three weeks from now."

She looked sheepish. "The truth is, we'd scheduled an anti-bullying assembly scheduled for that day but it's been postponed. You were such a hit with my students, Seretha—I mean Principal Herman—thinks you'll do an awesome job."

"Awesome, huh?" Max grinned. "I welcome the chance to share fire safety tips and information whenever I can. Let me run it by the captain and get back to you."

"You're a lifesaver." A dazzling smile lit her face.

He couldn't look away and for a moment lost himself in the warmth and welcome of her eyes. At the moment she seemed as into him as she had on the dance floor. Other times, not so much.

Her mixed messages confused him.

"I've never known anyone with blue-green eyes," he said. "Contact lenses?"

"They're natural. I don't know how I ended up with them. My mom has blue eyes and my dad's were dark brown."

"Were?"

"He passed away when I was twelve." She glanced at her hands.

"Bummer." Max's parents hated each other, which made for awkward and tense family get-togethers. Still, he was grateful that they were both around. "Did your mom remarry?"

She nodded. "Bennett's a really great guy. But even after twenty-one years I still miss my dad."

"I hear that. My parents are divorced and both very much alive, but I know what it feels like to lose a family member. I was nine when we lost my sister, Janet. She was seven."

Max didn't like to think of that unhappy time and never mentioned it. Wasn't sure why he'd brought it up now. It'd happened a long time ago.

Megan bit her lip. "I'm sorry. Do you mind my asking what happened?"

"She was riding her bike without a helmet. She hit a pothole, fell and banged her head on the pavement."

"I can't even imagine how awful that must have been."

"Yeah." Between the grief and his parents' split-up less than a year after the funeral, awful didn't begin to cover it.

To this day they hated the sight of each other. So much for love...

"Should we meet before the assembly and discuss what you want me to cover?" he asked.

"That's a great idea. We may as well set up a date and time now. What works best for you?"

Getting naked and under the sheets together, but Megan wasn't talking about that. Sometimes he was such a dog. Max stifled a self-derisive snicker. "How about after school the Friday before the assembly? That'll give me a week to prep."

"You sound like a teacher."

"As I said, training and workshops are part of the job. I don't do it day in and day out like you, but often enough. A few months ago I led my first in-house training. I enjoyed it so much that I've decided to apply to teach fire safety at the community college."

"You're going to teach a college class? I'm impressed."

"Save that for when they hire me. If."

"Why wouldn't they?"

"I've never taught the course. Way back when I took it, I graduated at the top of my class. A lot has changed since then, including the textbooks and DVDs, but I've kept up. That and my hands-on experience counts for a lot."

"Then they'd be crazy not to hire you."

"That's what I keep telling the captain. He's writing me a recommendation."

"Teaching won't conflict with your regular job?"

Max shook his head. "It's a three-hour seminar on Thursdays."

She raised one eyebrow, which intrigued him, and then she asked another question. "What's in-house training?"

"Firefighters need refresher courses, including chances to hone our skills. We also get information on new procedures and techniques. To keep up, we hold trainings three or four times a month. This year, I'm in charge of putting all that together." He couldn't help feeling proud.

"You really are busy."

"Better than being bored."

"It does make the time pass quickly," she agreed.

"When you came to Career Day you mentioned making custom furniture. I assume that doesn't figure in with your firefighting duties."

Max chuckled. "Nope."

She seemed genuinely interested, so he told her about his small business. "My dad is a mortgage broker, but his hobby is woodworking. His father taught him and he taught me."

Working alongside him in the basement was one of Max's fondest childhood memories. After Janet's death his father had banned him from that part of the basement, at a time when Max most needed him. He'd realized later that his dad had needed the space to grieve privately. Following his parents' divorce, Max had again joined his father in the shop at his new house.

"For him it's a hobby," he added. "I sell my

pieces. At the moment I'm working on a cabinet for a customer and thinking about the headboard I'll make for my crewmate, Adam, and his bride-to-be, Sam—for their wedding gift."

"Ava mentioned the cabinet yesterday. You're a man of many talents."

"I'm just a regular guy who's good with his hands."

Megan glanced at them and cleared her throat. "My dad was a birder. We spent a lot of family vacations bird-watching."

"Cool. Are you still into birds?"

"Not really. Our last few birding trips were no fun for anyone. I was getting to the age where I wanted to take 'normal' vacations like my friends, and I was surly and unhappy. Now I look back and cherish those times."

Megan's cell phone buzzed. "It's a text from Ingrid," she said. "She's wondering where I am." She glanced at her watch. "We've been sitting here quite a while."

Max hadn't even thought about the time. Talking to Megan was fun. So was trying to puzzle her out. Was she into him or not?

He meant to find out, sooner rather than later. He rose to his feet and offered her a hand up. "We should get back."

~

MAX SEEMED interested but who knew, Megan mused as they retraced their steps toward the bar and dance area. He certainly intrigued her. Everything he said made her want to know more about him.

And the warm way he looked at her... Staring at her as if she was candy and he needed sugar...

What sane woman could resist that?

She could.

Even if sitting within tempting reach of him had made the task more challenging. To Max's credit, despite his dirty-boy eyes he'd behaved himself. He hadn't laid a finger on her the whole time they'd shared the loveseat.

"You're awful quiet," he said as they rounded the corner toward the bathrooms.

His intent gaze set off a flurry of excitement inside. Good thing he couldn't read her mind.

"I'm thinking about Ingrid." She frowned at her watch while she got hold of herself. "If she's wasting her time wondering where I am, she and Tony must not—"

From out of nowhere, a man reeking of alcohol lurched toward her. "Hey, baby. I saw you on the dance floor earlier. Wanna dance?"

The men and woman waiting in the bathroom lines riveted their attention her way.

Max stepped between her and the drunk. "Watch it, buddy."

The guy's bloodshot eyes widened. "Didn't see you, man."

"You see me now. I hope you have a ride home tonight."

"With my friend. 'Scuse me." He disappeared through the door of the men's room.

Onlookers continued to watch her and Max with undisguised curiosity.

Ignoring them, he cupped her shoulders in his big hands and held her at arm's length. "You all right?"

No, but her shakiness had nothing to do with the drunk and everything to do with Max. Even with his paramedic's careful and impartial assessment of her, the chaos in certain body parts ratcheted to a fever pitch.

"I'm fine," she lied.

She meant to back away, only her legs got mixed up and brought her closer to him.

"Thanks," she added, without any idea what she was thanking him for.

No sign of professional paramedic now. His mesmerizing gaze settled on her mouth. Without any resistance at all, her lips parted on a needy sigh she couldn't repress any more than she could slow the rapid thud of her heart.

Grabbing her hand, he backtracked to the hall with the lounge area and pulled her into a recessed area behind a large potted plant. "Hey."

If ever there was a time to leave... Megan stayed right where she was. "What are you doing?"

"Oh, I think you know." He ran his thumb

over her bottom lip and let out a low laugh, and she forgot all about leaving. As he bent toward her, she met him halfway.

5
____

For once, Max had no problem reading Megan. She wanted this.

She wrapped her arms around his neck, anchoring him as her warm, soft mouth welcomed and encouraged. Her perfume, light and sweet as a breath of spring, filled his senses.

He broke off and buried his face in her soft hair. And caught the faint whiff of...baby? He pulled away.

With her dazed expression, loose hair wild around her face, and kiss-reddened lips, Megan looked aroused and very hot.

By all appearances, going in for more wouldn't pose a problem. First, Max needed to know. "You have a baby."

In the act of straightening her blouse, she shot him a startled look. "Where did you get that idea?"

"I know what babies smell like from when Ava was little. The scent is in your hair."

Frowning, she sniffed the air, then pulled a lock to her nose. "You're right. I never realized."

She still hadn't answered the question. "Do you have a boy or a girl?"

"Neither yet, but God willing, someday soon."

Looking horrified by her own revelation, she covered her mouth. "I shouldn't have said that. I mean, I hardly know you." One of her eyebrows tilted up, in what he was coming to recognize as a need for information. "Now that I have, do you have a problem with children?"

None, except being a father meant getting involved with the kid's mother and the inevitable heartbreak and loss when they split up. No, thanks. "As you saw in your classroom I like them fine. You must have spent time with a niece or nephew, or a friend's baby," he pressed, wondering why it mattered so much.

"I don't have any siblings and my cousins live in Montana. I haven't been around any friends' babies lately, either."

He scratched his head. "Maybe it's the shampoo."

"No. Let me text Ingrid so she doesn't worry. Then I'll explain."

Slipping out of the alcove, Megan typed a message. Max followed her.

Moments later she returned her phone to her purse and they started forward. "Now I'll tell you why my hair smells this way. This afternoon I cuddled a crack-addicted newborn for a couple of hours. I volunteer every Saturday."

Max wouldn't have guessed in a million years. She was full of surprises. "No kidding. Awhile back I saw a TV program about that. As I recall, the reporter profiled several volunteers, all senior citizens."

She nodded. "I watched the same piece. The very next day I called and offered to help. The hospital doesn't care whether I'm thirty or seventy. They're thankful to have me."

The music was louder now, and Max pulled her to a stop to finish the conversation. "I've never met anyone who did what you're doing," he said. "I'm impressed."

The whole idea of handling a helpless, little newborn, let alone one born addicted to drugs, made Max twitchy. Yet Megan gave them her time and attention on a regular basis.

"What's that like?" he asked.

"Heartbreaking, but also rewarding. It doesn't require much skill, just lots of love."

She seemed to have a big heart. "So you sit in a rocker with a baby and send out good vibes," he said.

"Exactly." Megan pantomimed holding an infant in her arms. "I want a child of my own. Until then, rocking the babies satisfies my nurturing needs."

"Don't you do that with Ava and the other kids you teach?"

"Yes, but it isn't enough."

"You must want a baby real bad."

She nodded. "First, I'd like to fall in love and get married."

Okay, then. Time to lay out his view on the subject, nice and clear. "Not me. I'm not into serious relationships or marriage."

"You mean not now."

"I mean ever." Short-term relationships where no one got hurt—that was his forte.

There went her eyebrow. "Mind if I ask why?"

"Because divorce sucks. It was rough for my parents and hell on my older sister Helen and me. I'm not putting myself or any kids through that. But hey, good luck."

"Thanks. I think."

"How long does it take for babies to get the drugs out of their system?"

"Every one is different, but they all require patience, love, and care. Most are agitated and unable to rest or nurse well.

"The little guy I was with today was especially miserable. When I arrived he hadn't slept or eaten in hours. Gentle rocking and soft words calmed him. When he wanted to eat I had the bottle ready."

The serene expression on Megan's face made Max's chest feel funny.

"After I burped him I rested my head against his," she said. "That has to be where I picked up his baby smell. From now on, I'll wash my hair before I go out on a Saturday night. Let's keep walking."

Max no longer heard music. "The band must be on break. Do you ever worry something might go wrong when you and the baby are alone?" he asked as they ambled forward.

"I did at first, but between the call button, the monitors sending information to the nurses, and the medical equipment within easy reach, I feel secure."

"I'll bet you get attached quickly."

"If I let myself, I would, but that's not a good idea. My sole purpose is to help a newborn get through drug withdrawal by offering love and security."

Max's admiration for her grew. "You don't shy away from the hard stuff, do you? That must take a lot out of you."

"And yet I keep going back."

What a woman. As drawn as Max was to her, they were as different as oil and water. She wanted marriage and kids. He didn't.

Ready to party with people who wanted a good time, period, he opened the swinging doors. "May as well get a fresh beer while I wait for the band." He nodded at Megan. "Good talking with you. I'll be in touch about the assembly."

~

READY TO GO HOME, Megan found Ingrid at their table. Her friend seemed equally glum. After donning their coats, they headed out the club's front door.

"What happened with you and Tony?" Megan asked, her breath clouding in the cold.

"He's okay."

"He's okay—that's it?"

Ingrid shrugged and unlocked her car. "He was friendly, but we didn't click."

Megan and Max certainly had—until she'd mentioned wanting to get married. "That's a shame," she said.

Ingrid's car rolled toward the exit, its headlights twin beams in the dimly lit lot.

"No big deal. I wasn't into Tony, and he wasn't into me. After a few dances, we went our separate ways. You and Max seemed to get along much better. You disappeared for quite a while."

Even in the dark, Megan caught her friend's speculative expression.

"It's not what you think. I wanted to talk to him about the assembly, and having a conversation on the loud dance floor is impossible. We found a place where we could hear each other."

"The only place I know of around here is the bathroom."

"This was way past the bathrooms, around the corner and down a hall. At the far end there are chairs and a couch."

"Who'd have guessed? You'll have to show me

sometime. That was one long conversation, though. I know you talked about more than the assembly."

"We did. I mentioned rocking crack-addicted babies."

"How did that come up?"

"He..." Megan broke off. "I'm not ready to talk about it."

"Now I'm intrigued. Go on."

Megan hesitated, then decided she may as well share. "All right, but don't judge."

"Me? Never."

"We covered a lot of ground—all that Max does as a firefighter, what I do, our families... He asked questions and listened as if what I said mattered. How many guys ever do that?"

"Lucky you." Ingrid frowned. "You had a good conversation. What's the big deal?"

"In the middle of it, he kissed me."

"Get out! I want details."

"I don't think so."

"No fair—I'm your BFF and things didn't work out with the hot guy I danced with. At least tell me if Max is a decent kisser."

"He is." Megan's lips still tingled.

"I knew it." Ingrid let out a dreamy sigh. "Your night was much better than mine."

"You haven't heard the whole story. Max said my hair smelled like baby."

Her friend's surprise was almost comical. "What?"

"You know the newborn I rocked today? Somehow his scent got in my hair. Max thought I had a baby at home."

"Seriously?"

"At my age I could. That's when I explained about rocking the babies."

"And?"

"He was impressed." Megan sucked on her bottom lip. "He's an amazing guy, but I shouldn't have let him kiss me this soon."

"Stuff happens. So you kissed and talked about your volunteer job."

"Yes, and..." Megan paused. "Do I have to tell you the rest?"

"Uh-huh."

"He had lots of questions about the babies, and I ended up telling him that I want a husband and kids."

"So? That's no big secret."

"No, but it came up a little earlier than usual and scared him off."

"You can't know that for sure. "

"Oh, no? As soon as I told him he pulled back." Max's interest and warmth had vanished as if she'd dreamed it. But his arms around her and his kisses had been real. "He also let me know that he doesn't want to get married. Ever. The second we reached the bar area we went our separate ways. It was over less than an hour after it started."

"At the beginning of a relationship, lots of guys feel like Max," Ingrid said.

"Relationship? We barely know each other. Anyway, he means it."

"He might not. Once you get better acquainted..."

"I'm not getting my hopes up," Megan said.

"You joined that online dating site, right?"

"Last night." Megan couldn't summon up much enthusiasm.

"Hey, give it a chance."

Ingrid pulled into the townhouse community where Megan lived and parked in front of her unit at the far end of the block. They hugged, then Megan slipped out of the car. Her friend tapped the horn in a friendly "good-bye" and left.

Inside, Megan greeted her coal black cat, Bling, named for his show-boy attitude that he should be showered in the stuff.

"Did you miss me?" she asked.

The purring feline butted her leg for attention. Megan indulged. "You don't care if I want to get married and have kids—you love me anyway," she said, stroking him. Then laughed at how pathetic she sounded. "As long as I fulfill your regal kitty needs."

Giving her a "you got that right" look, Bling turned away and hopped onto his favorite living room chair.

"Good night to you, too." Megan put on her pajamas, then padded to bed.

In the darkness and silence, she chastised herself for kissing Max before she knew a thing about what he wanted in a relationship. And thought about kissing him again. Which would never happen.

"Oh, well," she told herself.

Bling jumped onto the mattress, scooted to her side, and purred. In his own kitty way, he really did love her.

"There are more fish in the sea, and one of them is searching for me," she repeated for the cat's benefit—and to soothe her bleak heart.

The loud purring had softened to a murmur. Either Bling was in la-la land or he didn't for a second believe that fairytale.

"Or maybe not," Megan interpreted with a sigh. "Don't take this as a sign of giving up. I intend to try the dating site and stick with it till mid-June."

That settled, she closed her eyes and fell asleep.

6

———

As always at Monday morning breakfast, the entire team had gathered in the fire-house kitchen before the start of the double shift. While they ate, Max shared the homemade thank-you card waiting for him when he'd walked in. It had been signed by everyone, Ava and Megan included.

"They asked me back to do an all-student assembly," Max told Captain Comings. "I said I had to clear it with you."

The captain's brow furrowed. "I don't recall that you're scheduled for that."

"No prob—it'll be on a Friday."

"You're doing this on your own time?"

In other words, off the payroll. "That's right," Max said. "I've taught so many safety trainings for school-age kids, I could do this one in my sleep."

The captain gave his approval, and Max made a mental note to let Megan know. He felt pretty good.

Then Tony hooted. "If I were into Megan, I'd work for free, too."

"Who's Megan?" Hank asked with more interest than usual. Since he and Deanna had become a couple, he thought everyone should pair up.

That'd been Max's plan, but Megan's desire to fall in love and get married had put an end to that. "She's Ava's teacher," he said. "She saw how I connected with the kids and invited me to come back."

"There's more to the story than that," Tony said. "She likes you, and you like her—that was obvious when we ran into her at Lucky Joe's Saturday night. She's a honey."

Ethan grinned. "Even from the stage, the heat between you two almost lit the place on fire."

No arguments there. Max didn't want to get tangled up with her, but he thought a lot about her and those red-hot kisses.

"Wasn't long before she and Max took off. You two didn't come back for a long time." Tony winked. "You moved fast, buddy."

"It's not what you think," Max said. "We found a quiet place to talk about the assembly."

Tony snickered. "Great excuse for getting her alone. I'll have to remember that one."

"All right, I'm attracted to her," Max admitted. Strongly. "But she's not for me."

"A boyfriend, huh. She didn't come in with anyone."

"She's single, but she's looking to get married and start a family." Max rolled his eyes.

Ethan's jaw dropped. "She told you upfront? Most women don't bring that stuff up until later. She must want it bad. "

"At least I found out now," Max said. "Saves me problems down the road."

His single crewmates murmured agreement.

The captain, who'd been married forever and had heard various versions of the same conversation over and over, stood. "I need to clear a few things off my desk before this morning's meeting. See you in twenty." He glanced at Max. "Be ready with the rest of the month's in-house training schedule."

"I'll share what I've come up with, but we have room for more." Max's glance included all his teammates. "Keep those suggestions coming."

After stowing his gear in the little room where he bunked during his back-to-back shifts, he called Megan to update her about the assembly.

Her phone went to voice mail, a big disappointment. That puzzled him. He didn't want to go near her.

Rather than leave a message, he texted. Got the ok for the assembly.

That done, he headed to the apparatus bay on the lower level for the meeting.

〜

"Did you hear from Max?" Ingrid asked as Megan shouldered into her coat at the end of a long Monday.

"He texted. He'll do the assembly."

"That's good news, but I gotta be honest—a text doesn't sound promising."

"Didn't I tell you? Any interest he showed in me died as soon as I mentioned wanting to get married."

"What a shame."

"I agree, but it's better I found out right away than months into a relationship." As she had with Tyler.

"You've always been able to find the silver lining in life's challenges. Hmm... You have what? Two-plus weeks until the assembly? That gives us time to strategize."

"I'm not going to do that. If he's interested, he'll make the next move. If not..." Megan gave a dismissive wave. She didn't expect to hear from him until they met to finalize the details for the assembly. "Anyway, I happen to have a coffee date after work Thursday, with a guy from In the Cards."

"Good for you. What's his name?"

"Stuart. He's an industrial engineer. Six feet tall, blue eyes, and black hair. Divorced, no kids, but he'd like to remarry and start a family."

"Exactly what you want. He could be the man you've been looking for."

Megan was skeptical and not remotely excited about the man. Still, it couldn't hurt to try.

7

Worst. Date. Ever. As Stuart droned on about his ex-wife, Megan stifled a bored yawn. He probably wouldn't notice if she dozed off. Her herbal tea long gone, she fiddled with her empty mug. No sense getting a refill when she didn't plan on staying much longer.

What she'd hoped would be a promising first meeting had deteriorated the moment she'd laid eyes on Stuart. He'd lied about everything except for his age, hair, and eye color.

Megan measured five foot six in her stocking feet, and about three inches taller in the boots she'd worn. Instead of being six feet tall, Stuart stood eye level with her and was about thirty pounds overweight, most of the excess carried in his belly.

He was no industrial engineer, either. He worked as a sanitation engineer, aka a garbage truck driver.

She didn't care about that—honest work was honest work. But the ink had barely dried on his divorce papers, and he'd been pouring out the details since they'd sat down an eternity ago.

Like most men, Stuart expected the conversation to center around him. So different from Max's interest in her and what she had to say. And could he kiss. Megan couldn't even imagine kissing Stuart, not without gagging.

Stuart was still at it. "Then my attorney fired back and—"

Megan's eyes crossed. Refusing to waste one more second with him, she interrupted. "Excuse me. The Coffee Shack is closing soon and I need to get home."

Stuart went quiet. "This hasn't gone well, has it?"

When Megan shook her head, he let out a weighty sigh. "I guess it's too soon for me to date. Still, it was nice to talk to someone with a neutral opinion about my ex. I'll text you in a couple months, when I'm over her."

Megan fervently hoped he didn't.

She headed into the restroom. When she came out Stuart had gone. Yes!

"Plenty more fish in the sea," she murmured as she shrugged into her winter coat.

Her wayward thoughts returned to Max— which she needed to stop. Why engage in wishful dreams when he wasn't interested? He probably wasn't thinking about her at all.

The evening was clear and cold, and Megan's sedan was the only car left in the lot. She was barely out the door before the lone employee, a male who looked about twenty, put the "closed" sign in the window and cut most of the interior lights. He seemed as eager to get home as she was.

She was fishing the car key from her purse when an aging truck pulled into the lot and rolled up to the front door. The employee slipped through the door, locked up, and climbed into the passenger seat. Seconds later, the truck turned onto the highway and disappeared.

Anxious to do the same, Megan unlocked her car and slid in. The stubborn engine refused to start. "Don't fail me now," she begged. "I'm taking you to Al after work tomorrow. Please, please behave until then."

Cajoling didn't work. Neither did waiting a few minutes and trying again. After the third attempt she gave up and phoned AAA for a tow truck.

"We're real busy tonight," the dispatch lady said. "Must be the full moon. It'll be about an hour."

That long? Megan's stomach complained. It wanted food. Too bad the Coffee Shack was closed.

Did takeout places deliver to your car?

She was searching the food delivery options on her cell phone when a navy Ford Explorer

pulled into a nearby slot. In the driver's seat—
Max.

Of all people... But help had arrived, and she wasn't about to turn it down. Pretending she wasn't all excited, she smiled.

Max exited his car and headed toward her. Even in the long shadows cast by the perimeter lights he was gorgeous. Megan's heart lifted in admiration before she squelched that. No more of that.

On the plus side, she'd already laid her cards on the table. He knew what she wanted and wasn't interested, and she didn't need to be on her best behavior or worry about whether he'd ask her out. Which, given how hungry and tired she was, was a relief.

MAX HADN'T EXPECTED to run into Megan tonight, but the rush he got from seeing her came as no surprise. Few women knocked him off his feet the way she had the other night.

Getting involved would end badly, he told himself for the thousandth time. Leaning down, he knocked on her window.

She lowered it. "Hi."

"Hey. The Coffee Shack usually stays open till seven. They must've closed early."

"The one guy working here left almost fifteen minutes ago."

"He must've had plans tonight—a hot date or a party." Max shook his head. "Either way, I lose out on the vanilla latte I wanted."

"There are other places in town."

"Sure, but not as good as what they make here."

"Now I want one. If the Shack was still open, I'd go right in and order the decaf version."

"Not me—I'm a full-leaded guy." At the moment, turbo-charged.

"If I have caffeine after four, I'm up half the night."

"Never had that problem. So you've been sitting here for the last fifteen minutes. What's up with that?"

"My car won't start." Her loud exhale was pure frustration.

"It's good I came along. Your window works, so it's not the battery."

"That much I know. I've been having problems for over a week, but not consistently. I scheduled an appointment with my mechanic for after work tomorrow. I wish I'd gone in today instead of wasting my time with—" She cut herself off.

"Who?" Max asked, not happy at the thought of her with some other guy. Which was crazy. He had no claim on her and didn't want one.

"It's not important."

To Max it was, but he let the matter drop. He knew precious little about car troubles but figured he'd try. "I'm no engine expert and I don't have any tools with me, but I'll take a look. Pop the hood for me."

By the time he grabbed a flashlight from the Explorer and secured the car hood open with the hook prop, Megan had joined him.

Her coat was open and he glimpsed a dress and tights similar to what she'd worn the day he'd visited her class. She must've come here straight from school, meaning she'd been here awhile. Who had she been with?

In the cold night air, he caught a whiff of her breath-of-spring perfume. Instant, full-fledged turn-on, tough to ignore. Which was nuts, as he was not getting involved with her. She wanted marriage and the whole nine yards—he didn't. Simple as that.

He flashed his light around, checking a few things. Then shook his head. "Beats me. Could be the starter, a loose cable—anything." He shut the hood.

"At least you tried. Triple A promised to send a tow truck. They're super busy tonight, and it'll be about an hour."

"That's a long time to wait," Max said. Megan's stomach growled in agreement, and he grinned. "Especially when you're hungry."

"Starving. I haven't eaten since lunch. When you drove up I was searching the web for the restaurants willing to deliver to my car."

"Smart." Max's belly was also tilting toward empty. "What kind of food are you thinking?"

"I'd kill for a burger and fries, but I don't think fast-food places deliver."

"Sad but true. Now, Chicken D'Lite... They make a mean fried chicken, and their rolls and gravy..." He licked his lips at the thought. "I know where I'm eating tonight."

Right here, with Megan. Not the smartest idea, but he wasn't about to leave her stranded in the empty lot for God knew how long.

She laughed. "My mouth is already watering. I'm going to call them."

"Order me the full dinner with extra gravy and a soda."

The corners of her mouth turned down. "You don't have to keep me company."

"Maybe I want to." He stamped his feet. "It's cold out here. Your car or mine?"

She hesitated for a moment. "Yours, I guess."

She guessed? Forget he wasn't getting involved with her. What did she have against him?

The tow truck lumbered into the lot and he didn't get a chance to find out.

"Over here!" Megan waved her hands in the air. "That didn't take nearly as long as the dispatcher said. You don't have to hang around any more, Max."

"Someone has to drive you home after the tow truck drops the car at the mechanic's."

She groaned. "I hadn't even thought that far. Okay."

8

The tow truck deposited Megan's car at Al's Auto Repair, which had closed hours earlier. After collecting her purse and folders from the passenger seat, she placed the car key and a hastily scribbled note in an envelope and dropped it into the after-hours security box.

Once she deposited the folders in the back seat of Max's Explorer, he gave her a hand into the passenger seat.

He held onto her a moment longer than necessary. Heat flared in his eyes. There went her willpower. Her lips parted and she leaned toward him for a kiss.

But no, he released her and pivoted away.

She'd been mistaken. His touch and intent look had likely been products of her overactive imagination.

That had to be it. The attraction tonight was

hers and hers alone. And it kept growing by leaps.

What a colossal waste of energy and longing. This was why she ought to stay away from Max. Yet here she was, buckled into his car.

It's a ride home. Nothing to worry about.

"You sure have a lot of folders back there," he commented as he pulled onto the road.

"I gave a vocabulary test today and promised to grade it tonight and hand it back tomorrow. I also want to review tomorrow's lesson plan."

"New material?"

"No, but I want to revise a bit. I like to keep my students on their toes."

"I'll bet you do."

His eyes seemed to glitter in the darkness, the heat unmistakable. She hadn't imagined things, after all.

Her traitorous body warmed right up. She stared straight ahead. "To get to my house, turn right at the next intersection."

"No can do, not with Chicken D'Lite a couple miles straight ahead."

"You still want to eat there?"

"Don't you? They're fast and they always have an available table. I'll take you home after."

As hungry as she was, she needed to get away from Max. On the other hand, her empty stomach craved the chicken dinner.

Get away from Max as soon as possible, or fill

her stomach? Indecisive, she fiddled with her purse strap. "I don't know..."

"Hey, I don't bite. This is about food. I'm on empty and so are you."

Yes or no?

While she battled with herself, Max narrow-eyed her. "You've been cool toward me since I parked at the Coffee Shack. What's the deal?"

"I'll be thirty-three in a few months and I'd like to have a baby by age thirty-five."

Max pulled on his ear. "I'm not sure what you're trying to say."

"I can't afford to get sidetracked by you, no matter how much I want to."

"You like me." His wicked grin turned her inside out.

She gave a miserable nod.

He pulled into the strip mall where Chicken D'Lite was and jerked to a stop in an unlit slot far from the restaurant's door.

"There are lots of parking spaces closer to the restaurant," she said.

"First, I want to talk to you."

"Now, when food is so close and we're both running on empty?"

"Yep." His seatbelt clicked as he released the catch.

He swiveled toward her, looking like he wanted to inhale her. Her knees wobbled and she was glad to be sitting down. She glanced out the window, away from his irresistible gaze.

"We understand each other and that's good," he said. "But it doesn't change what is—that you like me and I like you. A lot. What are we going to do about it?"

Again with that hot, melting look. She swallowed hard. "Steer clear of each other."

"In the long term, but what about our mutual short-term, immediate needs?" He reached across the space between them and tipped up her chin. "I need to kiss you, and unless I'm mistaken you're right there with me."

She could no more deny that than stop breathing. "I am."

Letting out a low laugh, he followed through.

MAX HAD NEVER GIVEN the divider between the front seats a second thought, but now, after a sizzling kiss... He growled in frustration. "I can't get close to you the way I want."

Megan's eyes blinked open. With her hair awry and her lips parted, she was impossible to resist.

He went in for more, but she put her palm to his chest and stopped him. "This is close enough."

Not by a long shot, but it was too soon for what Max wanted—and a bad idea, to boot. He popped the locks on the doors. "Let's go eat."

Delivery service and takeout made up the bulk of business at the hole-in-the wall restaurant. He and Megan were the lone sit-down customers. Not long after they placed their orders at the counter and chose a table, the food arrived.

"OMG, this smells so good!" She rubbed her hands together like an excited kid.

Max grinned and they dug in, keeping conversation to a minimum while they devoured the meal.

"Feel better?" he asked as they finished up.

"Much. You?"

"Definitely." They bussed their dishes and headed out.

"How will you get to school tomorrow morning?" he asked on the way to the car. "Need a ride?"

"No, thanks. One of my fellow teachers lives near me. I'll ask her to pick me up."

They returned to the car, and Max drove toward her place. As much as he wanted her, the break in the restaurant had given him time to cool down.

"About this thing between us," he said.

"It stops now." She gave him a determined look. "I mean it, Max."

"I agree."

Clearly relieved, she sagged against the seat. "We should have talked about the assembly over dinner."

"Between the food and other things, it slipped my mind. We'll iron out the details at our meeting. A week from tomorrow after school, right?"

She nodded. "Come to my classroom."

He pulled up to her place, a modern, two-story unit on the corner of a well-kept townhouse community, and started to get out.

"Don't bother," she said.

"If your house lights were on, I wouldn't. This is a safety thing."

"Don't be silly. Most of my neighbors are home. If my coffee date hadn't run late... I never expected to be out this late. It's no big deal."

"To me, it is. You never said what happened at the Coffee Shack—except for calling it a waste of time."

"A huge waste," she corrected. "And not worth talking about."

"Indulge me," he said as they sauntered toward her front steps.

"All right. In three words, online dating sucks."

"So I hear."

She gave him an unreadable look. "You've probably never had to stoop to paying a dating service to get a date."

"Once or twice I thought about it, but my sister tried a couple times and struck out. Same thing happened to a couple of my crewmates. Why are you doing it?"

She gaped at him as if the answer was obvious. "Because it's a good way to meet marriage-minded men who want to start a new family."

Max had his doubts. He frowned. "I wouldn't trust that. Some guys will say anything for sex."

"That won't work on me. I don't sleep with a guy until I get to know him. Online dating may turn out to be a waste of time, but for the sake of my biological clock I have to try."

She set her things on a wicker table on her front porch. Max took her phone and shone the flashlight in her purse while she rifled through it for the key.

"You have a lot of stuff in that purse. It must weigh a ton."

"Believe me, I need everything in here."

"If you say so. When is your next date?" he asked, striving to keep his tone neutral. None of his business, but he wanted to know.

"Saturday morning, and two more lined up after school next week."

No surprise there. A woman as pretty as Megan was sure to draw plenty of guys. Nothing Max could do about that. He didn't have the right. All the same, he didn't like it. He set his jaw and handed over her phone. "Be careful."

"Always. It's not like I haven't done this before."

Max heard a plaintive meow through the door. "You have a cat."

She nodded. "I adopted him from Cat Rescue."

"I know that place—they find good homes for strays."

"And I got a great tom—Bling."

"Bling?" Max chuckled.

"The name suits him to a tee. You wouldn't believe the sparklies he brings home—broken earrings and jewelry, scraps of glittery wrapping paper and ribbon. He's worse than a dog."

Max wanted a look at the animal but Megan didn't invite him in.

She unlocked her door, then scooped up her stuff. "Thanks for everything."

"Everything?"

Her eyes darkened and her lips parted a tempting fraction in silent plea for a good-night kiss. The haze of lust he'd battled all too often lately blindsided him once more. But they'd agreed to back away.

As he shoved his hands in his jacket pockets, Megan jerked toward the door and opened it.

"Good night." She slipped inside and bolted the lock behind her. As if that could protect her from the hunger gnawing at them both.

The porch light flickered on, lighting Max's way down the steps. His body hard and hungry for her, he strode to his car. For both their sakes, they should avoid being alone together.

What about their meeting next week? Too many people around school, and if her classroom door remained open... That'd work.

Hell, the meeting wasn't for another eight days. By then surely a disciplined guy like him ought to be able to get hold of himself.

No sweat. Max relaxed. Yet all the way home, he thought about her.

9

_____

"**Y**our ignition switch is bad," Al explained when Megan called him from school Friday morning.

Max had mentioned that possibility. She considered letting him know. Better not. Not with her strong feelings for him. Distance, then. No contact except for the meeting about the assembly. Then at the assembly, a brief "It's been nice knowing you" and good-bye.

"How long will it take long to fix?" she asked.

"You're in luck—I have the part and the time to work on it this afternoon. It'll be ready by closing today."

"Wonderful."

Ingrid had already offered her a ride home. Megan was sure she wouldn't mind dropping her off at Al's instead. Megan looked forward to that —she needed to talk privately with her friend, an all but impossible feat during a busy school day.

When the dismissal bell rang and the building emptied, she tidied her room and set out what she needed for Monday. Ingrid finished her routine around the same time and they strolled out of the building.

In the frigid air, Megan shivered. "I'm so tired of winter."

"And the flu bug that seems to have come with it," Ingrid said. "I had three kids out sick today."

"Two in my classroom. Let's hope it passes quickly."

On the way to the car, they discussed more of the goings-on in school.

As they buckled up, Ingrid glanced at her. "You haven't said a word about the date with Stuart."

So much had happened with Max, Megan had almost forgotten about that. "It was a total waste." She launched into the details. "You know what happened with my car—it wouldn't start," she finished. "By then the guy at the Coffee Shack had locked up and gone, a whole fifteen minutes early."

"That wasn't nice."

"Max didn't think so, either."

"Wait—Max saw you with your date?"

Wouldn't that have been interesting... Megan shook her head. "He came later to get a vanilla latte. There I was, the only car in the lot, waiting for the tow truck."

"Kismet." Ingrid sighed. "I love when that happens."

"I wouldn't exactly call a stalled car and a guy looking for a latte kismet."

"Oh, no? Max could have gone anyplace for his coffee, but he chose the Shack. You also ran into each other at Lucky Joe's. Sounds like kismet to me."

Megan scoffed. "You're such a romantic."

"You used to be."

"And look where it got me—nowhere. I'm not even close to meeting my forever guy."

"Max could be the one."

"I wish."

"Things went badly in the parking lot?"

"The opposite—he waited with me for the tow truck, followed it to Al's, and then gave me a ride after." Wowing her with his good-guy charm.

"Your own hero."

"I was all alone in a dark parking lot—he didn't have much choice." Never mind that he'd gone above and beyond later. "We didn't leave Al's until almost eight. By then we were both starving, so we stopped at Chicken D'Lite."

"I love that place! Kinda sounds like a date."

"It wasn't." Megan let out a heavy sigh

Her friend gave her a shrewd look. "You're holding back on me."

"You know me too well. All right, I'll tell you. He kissed me again." Making her want dangerous things.

"And you thought you scared him away. Anything else?"

Besides turning her brain to mush? "That's all."

Thanks to the divider between the seats. Without it, who knew what would have happened.

"A bad blind date, a stalled car, then dinner and a kiss from one of the sexiest guys in town—talk about a spectacular finish to the evening. In your shoes, I'd be doing a happy dance. But you... Why the glum face?"

"There's no point getting excited when it's never going to happen again."

"Bet you a cocktail you're wrong."

"You'll lose. We want different things."

"Which you both already knew. You still kissed each other."

"And we agreed to stop. I'm going to keep my eye on the ball. Anyway, when I got home last night, I checked my In the Cards account. There were at least half a dozen requests to meet."

"That sounds promising."

"Not if you read the profiles. I can't get excited about any of them."

"You're sure to get tons more requests."

"Who cares? The date with Stuart reminded me how awful online dating is. I've never met anyone I liked that way. Max's sister and his friends haven't had much luck, either."

"You told Max about In the Cards?"

"Why wouldn't I? We'll never get together."

"Good point. You were going to give In the Cards six months, but I think you changed your mind."

"I have. Still, I paid for a nonrefundable, one-month trial membership and I want my money's worth. Besides, I don't have any better options." Megan squared her shoulders. "I'll give those profiles another look."

"I would. We're almost at Al's."

"That didn't take long. Thanks for the ride. Hey, do you want to meet for dinner and then see a movie Saturday night?"

"Can't—I have a date."

This was news. "With James or someone new?"

"New. His name is Logan. We met Sunday afternoon in a coffee line, of all things."

Megan gaped at her. "That was almost a week ago, and you're just now telling me?"

"You know how hectic things are at school, especially with so many kids out sick. I had meetings with several parents after school, and you've been busy, too. We haven't even walked to our cars together.

"Back to Logan. We both intended to run into the Coffee Shack, pick up coffee, and go. Instead, we ended up at a table. We chatted for almost an hour, and he's called every night since. We have so much to talk about."

"That's amazing," Megan said.

"I know. You'll never guess what he does for a living—he's a wine importer. He's almost six feet tall with light brown hair and a great smile." Ingrid offered a happy smile of her own.

"Where is he taking you tomorrow night?"

"Out for dinner and drinks. I can't wait."

"You never have a problem meeting guys. I'm jealous," Megan admitted.

"It's easy, when getting married and starting a family aren't at the top of the agenda."

SATURDAY AFTERNOON, Max's sister Helen, a bookkeeper at a health food co-op, had to work. Their mother, who often watched Ava, had plans, and their father and his wife were out of town, so Max volunteered.

"Okay with you if I take her ice skating and then to The Rogue for a milkshake?" he asked Helen. Two of Ava's favorite activities.

His sister nodded, but his niece shook her head. "I'm too tired, Uncle Max."

She did look pale and exhausted. He frowned. "You feeling all right?"

"That sleepover she went to last night kept her up late," Helen explained.

"We'll do it another time," Max said. "Go take a nap."

His weary niece dragged herself to her room.

As soon as the bedroom door closed, he spoke to Helen in a voice too low to carry. "I need to run something by you about Ava's birthday gift." Next month she turned nine.

He'd finished the cabinet for his customer. The reclaimed wood slabs he'd ordered for Adam and Sam's headboard would arrive sometime next week, giving him a small window of time to focus on his niece's present.

Helen looked thoughtful. "Well, she's really into horses. I'm giving her riding lessons, Mom plans to buy her riding boots, and Dad already bought her a model horse kit. Hmm..."

"I know what I'm giving her," Max said, visualizing the pretty chunk of apple wood he'd been saving. "A handcrafted jewelry box."

"She'll love that. Of course, she doesn't own any good jewelry yet, but she has a few little treasures to store."

While Helen was gone Max did a preliminary sketch of the box he had in mind. Not too small or girlie—he wanted something Ava could use for a long time.

When Helen returned, he'd head for Bigelow's Arts & Crafts on the opposite side of town and check out hinges and other hardware.

That decided and Ava still asleep, he surfed the 'net. He didn't think about Megan at all—not much, anyway. She'd had a coffee date this morning. What if she liked the guy and they started something? Max scowled at the idea, then caught himself.

All the better for him if she did. But the thought put him in a foul mood.

10

After yet one more bad date followed by two hours with a crack-addicted baby no amount of rocking had calmed, Megan needed something to brighten her Saturday. She knew just the thing—a trip to Bigelow's to pick up supplies for a school art project. Browsing through the store was great fun.

As usual on a weekend afternoon the store was crowded with crafts enthusiasts. Determined to throw off her gloom, Megan put on a happy face and began a leisurely stroll through the aisles.

Smiling and trading comments with other shoppers did wonders for her mood—that and loading her cart with needed supplies and those she'd never realized she wanted. But hey, if it boosted her spirits...

Feeling like her normal, upbeat self, she stopped to explore the miniatures, one of her favorite sections in the store. Shelves and bins of tiny figures of men, women, children, animals, trees, vehicles, houses, and other buildings— everything a person could possibly imagine to create a family, a neighborhood, and a small town.

A little paint, carefully placed decorations, and... Megan's imagination bloomed with possibilities. Someday when she had a child of her own, they would come here and choose pieces together.

Provided she ever had a son or daughter. The way things were going, she couldn't help but wonder.

And there went her morale. Refusing to give up hope, Megan raised her head. Her forever guy was out there and sooner or later she'd find him.

Drawn by some irresistible force, she homed in on an imposing male at the far end of the aisle. His back was to her, but his short brown hair, extra-broad shoulders, long legs, and sexy butt were easily recognizable. Max.

Megan pulled the cart to an abrupt stop. Of all people, she'd never imagined running into him here. Looking dreamy in a weathered leather jacket and faded jeans, he pawed through a bin with studied concentration.

Simply staring at him was sheer pleasure. Nearby, two women around her age caught her admiring sigh and followed her gaze.

"Whew," one breathed. "That's one gorgeous hunk of man."

As if sensing Megan's stare, Max swiveled his head her way. A grin that wrinkled the corners of his eyes lit his face, taking her breath away. He started toward her with his fluid stride.

"Lucky you," the same woman murmured.

Megan didn't know whether the woman stuck around or moved off. She was riveted on Max.

"Hi," she said, relieved that she sounded normal. "I never expected to see you here."

"Ditto." He looked her over with the dark-eyed warmth that set her body thrumming.

And here she was, dressed in a bulky parka and the old slacks and soft, cotton pullover she wore to rock the babies.

"Did you get your car fixed?"

She nodded. "Al had it ready by the time school ended yesterday."

"He works fast. What was wrong with it?"

"One of the things you suspected—a bad ignition switch."

He nodded. "I'll bet you're relieved to have it back in time for the weekend."

"For sure. Which reminds me—I offered to hand out Al's business card. You might need his services someday. Will you take one?"

"Why not."

She pulled a card from her purse and handed it over. Her fingers barely skimmed Max's, but the damage was done. The familiar ache for a more intimate touch clamored through her. She picked up a plain wood stop sign, then put it back.

"It's weird how we keep running into each other," she said. "First at Lucky Joe's, then the Coffee Shack, now here."

"In small towns, that happens a lot."

"Not with us until lately. Maybe we didn't see each other before because we hadn't met." As if. How could any woman with eyes fail to see Max?

"Trust me, I'd have noticed you."

Another very warm look. Did he have any idea what he did to her?

Megan brushed a speck of lint from her jacket sleeve. "Ingrid says it's kismet when two people meet each other this often in unexpected places."

"Fate?" Max snorted. "I don't subscribe to that."

"Oh, I don't know…"

"You're a believer."

"Not so much anymore, but the possibility has always intrigued me. And it does make you stop and think. I mean, why is it happening with us?"

He glanced at her mouth. "Chemistry."

Which was no answer at all. "What does that have to do with our running into each other?"

"Hell if I know."

He grinned again and her body trembled. Her attraction to him was definitely growing. She straightened the items in her cart.

"You found a lot of stuff today," Max commented.

"More than I intended. I came here to buy

supplies for a school project and got sidetracked with ideas for myself."

"I do that with wood. I always end up with stuff I can use later. What's the project?"

"Self-portraits. I'm always surprised at how my students view themselves."

"Sounds interesting. I wonder what Ava will come up with."

"They'll be framed and hung in the classroom by Friday. You'll see it then." Megan gestured at the shelves. "Are you looking for miniatures?"

Max shook his head. "Scouting out things for Ava's birthday present."

"Is her birthday coming up? I didn't realize."

"At the end of next month. I'm designing a custom jewelry box for her."

"Wouldn't it be easier to buy one instead?"

"I'd rather make her something she can keep. I'm scoping out hardware—hinges, latches, knobs."

"And you're looking here."

"Plus a couple supply catalogues and online sites. For what I have in mind, I want something special."

"Such as?"

"Haven't figured that out yet, but I'll know it when I see it. The next aisle has more stuff. Why don't you help me look?"

Pleased, Megan smiled. "Sure."

"How was your date this morning?" Max asked.

His slightly narrowed eyes gave no indication what he was thinking. Megan made a face that lightened his expression.

"That bad, huh? Which date was worse—the one this morning or the other night?"

"They were equally awful. The man today claimed to be thirty-six. I liked his profile photo, but it must have been taken when he really was that age. He's at least fifty and quite a bit heavier. With a combover."

At the time it hadn't seemed funny, but sharing with Max made her giggle.

His lips quirked. "At least you're smiling."

"It's either that or cry. And it does make for a good story."

"There is that."

"I'm going to report him to the site so others don't waste their time."

They stopped in front of a bin. Max picked up several hinges and spread them across his big palm. "What do you think of these?"

Megan got lost in the sheer size of his hand. He had calluses on his palm and fingers. She imagined him touching her most sensitive parts with those work-roughened hands... Her nipples hardened.

Want to or not, she had a bad case of the hots. She cleared her throat. "I can't choose—I don't have any imagination about this kind of thing."

"I'll show you what I have in mind. This is a preliminary sketch."

He dug into his pocket, causing the shoulders of his leather jacket to strain at the seams.

There went her knees. She quickly forgot about that when he brought out a folded sheet of paper and opened it. The clean, elegant design impressed her. "This is really pretty, Max. Ava will love it."

"That's what my sister said. I'll be using apple wood, which is hard, durable, and beautiful."

He looked at her as if he thought she was beautiful, tumbling her insides into a frenzy.

Focus on the conversation. "I don't think I've ever seen apple wood, except on a tree in an orchard."

"Which is exactly where I picked up this piece—from a grower who thinned out his stand. I happen to have a photo." He called up images on his phone.

Standing close with his head bent, he shared the special features of the wood in a low, intimate tone. His lips almost grazed her ear like a lover's.

A wave of longing washed over her. To be his lover.

What was the matter with her? She inched away. "I-it's nice," she stammered, "but all I see is a hunk of wood."

"You wait—I'll turn it into something special."

Of that, Megan had no doubts. "Maybe Ava will bring it to school and show it off. I still can't help you with the hinges."

"No prob—I'll refine the sketch and think

more about this." He nodded at her cart. "What else are you looking for?"

"Not a thing. I found exactly what I need."

"You sure about that?" Max's hooded eyes gave her words a whole new meaning.

For one endless, charged moment, they communicated solely through their locked gazes, a silent, mutual yearning. The arc between them so vital and magnetic, Megan could almost reach out and grab it. Grab him.

"Gotta go. 'Bye." Gripping the handle of the cart, she executed a U-turn.

She wheeled away as fast as she could go, almost running toward the checkout area.

STUNNED. That about summed up Max's state of mind as Megan disappeared into the crowd at Bigelow's. She'd turned him upside down.

He frowned at the piece of paper that had fallen from her purse. A shopping list. Hardly aware of his actions, he stuffed it into his pocket.

Deep in thought and empty-handed, he headed for the exit. The conversation between him and Megan had been harmless enough, but the nonverbal stuff... Difficult to ignore the powerful pull between them.

Yeah, they were wrong for each other, but forgetting her and moving on was proving impossible. Max wanted to get to know her, wanted her under him, crying out in pleasure.

He started to get hard. Shaking his head and in need of a serious distraction, he headed for his car. The sun was sinking and darkness was descending, but his plans for the evening, meeting Tony and Rob at the pool hall, wouldn't be for hours yet. May as well head home, re-sketch, and cull through supply catalogues.

And what do you know, he found himself parked in front of Megan's.

"This is a bad idea," he muttered as he headed for the porch.

Unlike the night he'd dropped her off at a dark house, this time cheerful light blazed behind the curtained windows. From inside he heard music, something mellow and folksy.

Moments after he rang the bell, she opened the door. Wearing a Kiss the Cook apron and a smudge of flour on her cheek, with her hair pulled back but coming loose, she looked cute and hot at the same time.

"Max." Looking surprised, she tightened her hair tie.

"What're you making?" he asked.

"Bread. I like to bake."

She cooked, too? His mouth watered. "If you're looking for someone to sample the finished product, I'm your guy." He wiped his feet on the mat. "Gonna let me in?"

She opened the door wider. "The dough has

to rise twice before it's ready for the oven, about an hour and a half from now. We just saw each other at Bigelow's."

He stepped into the small entry and shut the door behind himself. Glanced at the colorful living room beyond the entry, then pulled her list from his pocket. "You dropped this."

"I wondered what happened to that." She tucked the paper into an apron pocket.

"You have flour on your face." Max gestured at her cheek.

As she brushed at it, a plaintive "meow" mingled with the music and a large black cat stalked toward them.

"You must be Bling." Hunkering down, Max greeted the tom. "Come here, big guy."

One pat and the animal turned into a purr machine. When Max straightened, Bling padded off.

He shrugged out of his jacket and laid it on the bench in the entry.

"You're planning to stay?" Megan said.

Did she have to look so unhappy? "I drove all the way over here to bring you that shopping list, and all I get is a frown?"

"You could have thrown it away."

"How was I supposed to know that?"

"Because I'd crossed off every item? You have my number. A call or a text would have saved you the trip."

His turn to scowl. She caught her bottom lip

between her teeth, then released it. "That was rude. I apologize."

He was so captivated by her mouth, he didn't reply.

"Don't tell me I still have flour on my face." Megan rubbed her hand across her cheeks and over her luscious lips. "Let's rewind to when you first handed me the list. You're very thoughtful to return this, Max. Why don't you take your jacket off and stay for a while? Can I get you a glass of wine or a beer?"

"Much better." He shook his head. "I have something else in mind."

"You mean food?"

"No—this." He cupped her shoulders and kissed her, holding himself in check until she let out a soft sigh and sank against him. The sweetest yes ever.

"God, you taste good," he said when he came up for air.

"Probably the chocolate bar I ate on the way home."

He kissed her again. "Nope, no chocolate. You have the sexiest mouth."

Ready for more, he lowered his head. Bling bumped his shin. Holding tight to Megan, Max eyed the cat. "Your timing sucks, big guy."

"Let him wait. Kiss me again." Megan tugged Max's head down.

Devouring the lips he couldn't get enough of, he backed her to the living room couch. "Where did we leave off?" he said, keeping her close when they sat down.

"I believe your tongue was in my mouth."

She plastered herself against him, and for a long time neither of them spoke. Easing her back he cupped her breasts. She moaned and he gave a low growl. "Yeah, I like that, too. Why don't you get rid of your apron."

As soon as she did, he unbuttoned her shirt and cupped her through her bra. Her nipples sharpened and she thrust up into his palm.

On the verge of losing his mind, he wanted only to get naked with her. First they should talk. He tore his mouth away from hers.

Flushed and unfocused, she looked bewildered. "Why did you stop, Max?"

"The other night we both agreed this wouldn't happen. But every time we're together... See what you do to me?" He nodded at his tented fly. "I've been this way since Bigelow's. I've tried my damnedest to fight this attraction to you, but I'm losing the battle. I want you and you want me just as bad."

Megan buttoned her blouse. "I never felt like this before. One look from you—heck, the slightest hint of a smile—and I'm lost." She drew her knees close and hugged them as if trying to protect herself. "Even when you're not around, I dream about you. About us. Running into each other all the time doesn't help."

"I hear that loud and clear, but this crazy heat

between us changes nothing. If you're looking for a lifetime commitment from me, you're in for disappointment."

"Yes, I know." Her hair had come loose and she tucked it behind her ears.

"You're open and ready for love. You should be with a man who can give you what you want and deserve." Max meant that. If the thought of some other guy loving her tore at him, too bad.

"What if I don't care about that right now?"

"When you cool down you'll feel different."

"Probably." She blew out a heavy sigh and ducked his gaze.

And that seemed to be the end of the conversation.

"I'm meeting a couple of my buds soon. I'd best go." Max rose and offered her a hand up.

In the entry, he pulled on his jacket and nodded at Bling. "Take it easy, big guy. Night, Megan."

"Good night."

As he crossed the yard, he glanced back at her. Clutching Bling, she stood in the threshold of the open door. With her hair brushing her shoulders and light spilling around her, she was any red-blooded male's dream woman.

Beautiful, desirable, and willing. But not his —now or ever.

In the darkness, he trudged to his car.

11

"**Y**our game is way off tonight, Max," Tony pointed out at the pool hall where Max met him and Rob.

"Yeah, you're a million miles away," Rob said. "What's with you?"

Max took a swig of his beer before answering. "I saw Megan today."

About to take a shot, Tony gave a smug grin. "You're into her."

"She's into me, too." Which made it that much harder to leave her earlier. Emphasis on hard.

Tony frowned. "So what are you doing here with us?"

"Like I told you before, she wants the white picket fence and kids."

"Yeah, but she knows where you stand. If she's interested anyway..." Tony aimed and executed a perfect shot. "I'm da man!" he crowed, polishing his fingernails on his shirt. "Wait—is she one of those women who figures that with time and patience she can bring you around to her point of view?"

Maybe at first, but now? Max shook his head. "She gets me loud and clear."

"Then I repeat, why are you hanging out with us?"

"I don't want to hurt her."

The corner of Rob's mouth lifted. "You like her a lot."

Max did, but not as much as she wanted him to. He glared at Rob. "And your point is?"

"Just sayin'."

Tony finally missed a shot. Max cued up, bent over the table, and studied the possibilities with a critical eye. For all the good that did. He missed the pocket by a mile.

Shaking his head, he hung up his cue. "That's it for me—I'm outta here."

THE POSSIBILITY of a serious relationship with Max was zero and no amount of wishing for a different outcome would alter that. Getting involved with him would delay Megan's chances of finding her forever guy anytime soon and all but guaranteed heartache.

Her brain knew that. The trouble was, desire for him trumped her logic. She spent a restless weekend of indecision. Satisfy her overpowering desire for Max or run the other way? She was still struggling on Monday.

"You haven't even asked about my date Saturday night," Ingrid commented as they headed through the parking lot after school.

Immersed in her own problems, Megan had forgotten about that. "Tell me," she said, feeling guilty for being so self-involved. "How did it go?"

"Really well. We're going out again Friday night. How were your dates?"

Megan hadn't that a second thought. She groaned. "Terrible."

"Both of them?"

"I only had one."

"Don't tell me the other man cancelled."

"I did." Mainly because the thought of making small talk with a stranger had been too much to bear, especially when she was so preoccupied with Max.

"But you said... I thought you were going into this thing full tilt," Ingrid said.

"That was the plan but I hit a snag. I ran into Max at Bigelow's Saturday."

Her friend's eyes widened. "I never pictured him as the arts and crafts type."

"I was surprised, too. He's designing a jewelry box for Ava's birthday—he makes custom wood pieces—and wanted to look at decorative hinges and fasteners. He showed me the sketch he made of Ava's box. You should see it. He's talented."

"I'm sure he is, in many ways."

More than Ingrid would ever know. Even now, two days after their steamy afternoon, Megan was on fire. She pulled her friend to a stop. "I need to tell you something, but I don't want it getting around."

Her friend pantomimed zipping her lips. Although Megan detected no one else within listening distance, she leaned in and lowered her voice. "We went our separate ways, or so I thought. Not long after I got home, he came over."

"Ooh. And?"

"Let's just say he left before things got too hot and heavy."

"You sent him away." Ingrid gave a sage nod and they resumed walking.

Megan shook her head. "Leaving was his decision. I—"

"Hold it right there. Are you telling me you wanted him to stay?"

"More than anything. He didn't think that was a good idea and it wasn't. He is absolutely, positively not interested in a serious relationship, let alone marriage and kids. For my sake, I have to move on. That's what I keep telling myself, but I can't even look at another man right now. Pretty sad, huh?"

"Hey, you feel how you feel. It's like that old song, 'Fever.' " Snapping her fingers, Ingrid belted out a few bars. " 'You give me fever, fever when you kiss me, fever when you hold me tight.' "

"You can't hold a tune worth beans," Megan teased, "but the words definitely fit. He's coming to school Friday to finalize details for next week's assembly. How am I supposed to get through that?"

"You do have it bad. What do you want to do?"

"Aargh! I don't know. I want to get married, but I also want to be with Max."

"I see two options. One, treat him as you would any adult professional and focus on the program, which you'll do anyway. Also be sure to make plans for after work so you won't be tempted to spend the evening with him. Or two, indulge yourself and get him out of your system. Then go back to searching for a marriage-minded guy."

The second option was tempting, but... "The problem is, I like Max way too much. Sex will only complicate matters."

"From everything you told me, they're already complicated."

True. "Sex is a big deal. I need to think about it."

"Isn't that what you've been doing nonstop?"

Megan rolled her eyes. "You're no help at all. But thanks for the input."

Ingrid flashed a breezy grin. "Any time."

12

A s the clock ticked toward the end of the school day Friday, Megan lapsed into a confusing state of anticipation and dread. In less than an hour, Max would be here. Taking Ingrid's suggestions to heart—one of them, anyway—she'd made plans for the evening. Plans that didn't include Max.

She was not going to have sex with him, or kiss, touch, or anything but focus on the assembly. Which wouldn't protect her from herself. The merest glance from him sent dangerous feelings skyrocketing through her. How could she possibly fight something that strong?

If I want marriage and a family of my own in the near future, I have to. The reminder helped, and by the time the students had left the building she'd mentally rolled up her sleeves to get through the meeting without a hitch and send Max on his way.

As she tidied the room, Ingrid poked her head in. "Logan is picking me up at five and I have to scoot. All set for Max?"

"For the meeting. That's all that will happen, period."

"All right. That's probably smart." As Ingrid turned to leave she nearly collided with Max.

Big and badass as always he steadied her and grinned. "Careful, there."

He wasn't even looking at Megan. All the same her wayward heart lifted and every atom in her body perked up.

"Hello and good-bye," Ingrid said. "Everyone is excited about your assembly next week."

"I'll do my best to satisfy."

He would use that word.

He stepped through the door. Suddenly the classroom seemed a lot smaller.

"How are you?" he asked.

Fine, thanks. The words hovered on the tip of her tongue, but why lie? "You want the truth? This is awkward for me."

"Because of what happened Saturday?"

"Because of how I acted."

"You liked what we did. Me, too."

His warm gaze darted over her. Her nipples contracted, and further south an ache bloomed. She crossed her arms. "I don't want to want you."

"First time I ever heard that."

"You know what I mean, Max."

He sobered. "Yeah—hands off."

He swiveled his head around the room, looking at the artwork tacked on the wall. "So those are the self-portraits. You said they'd be interesting and they are. Which one is Ava's?"

"See if you can find it without looking at the names."

He stood in front of the wall, finally pointing at one of the drawings. "This one has to be Ava's. I get the freckles and yellow hair, but what's with the black eyelashes and the tiger she's riding?"

Megan laughed. "I have no idea, but I think the tiger has to do with a movie she saw. I don't know about the lashes, though. You'll have to ask her."

"I will."

"She's had a rough week," Megan said. "Today was especially bad. She was out of sorts and seemed exhausted. I sent her to the nurse but she didn't have fever. She insisted on coming back to finish the day in the classroom."

"She loves school. Before I saw you Saturday I was over at Helen's. Ava had been at a sleepover and was tired then, too. Either she hasn't caught up on her rest or she's coming down with something."

"Let's hope she hasn't caught the nasty flu that's going around." Megan pulled a folding chair from the room's supply closet and set it up across the desk. "I don't want to keep you. Shall we get started?"

Max sat down. "You mentioned the assembly

should last ninety minutes and the whole school will attend," he said. "What else do I need to know?"

"There are huge differences between ages five and fourteen. Your biggest challenge will be to engage everyone."

"I've been thinking about that. Humor and true stories work for kids of all ages. People are always interested in my turnout gear."

Especially when the firefighter delivering the information was as buff and handsome as Max.

"I'll bring some of the equipment we use to fight fires, including my SCBA or self-contained breathing apparatus, aka air pack, and demo how to use it. To make things fun, I'll run a contest to see which class correctly guesses the weight of all my gear. The winning class will get a tour of the station."

"Our students will love that. Before you go, I'll show you the auditorium."

He sat back. "That's it—the meeting's over?"

"I should've known you'd come prepared. We could have done this over the phone and saved you the trip." And her the stress. Why hadn't she thought of that?

"I had to drive out here anyway for tonight's poker game."

"You play poker?"

"Unless I have other plans. It's a standing Friday night game for the crew and anyone else from the station. We take turns hosting."

Megan pictured a group of hotties in all their testosterone-filled gorgeousness around a table and fought the urge to fan herself. "I suppose you smoke cigars and drink beer."

"And eat junk food. Is there any other way to play poker? We also play for money."

"Then it's serious."

"Serious good times. Each player tosses a quarter into the kitty, so the pot never gets bigger than a few dollars. But winning is always sweet. I should know—I've won the last four games."

He looked so pleased with himself that she laughed. "Smart aleck."

"Just callin' it like it is."

She shook her head, then made a show of checking her watch.

"No rush—I don't have to be there for a while yet."

"You're not the only one with plans." She stood.

Expression shuttered, he rose beside her. "Something fun?"

"I wouldn't call having dinner at my mom and stepdad's fun, but it'll be nice."

He nodded, nothing changing except a subtle easing in his shoulders. They started down the hall. "I'm overdue to visit my parents—both sets," he said.

"I'm guessing they're all nearby."

"Unfortunately. My mom and her husband live on the south side and Dad and his wife are up north—about as far as they can get and still live in town."

"You don't get along with them?"

"I have no problems with either one. What I can't stand is that they detest each other."

" 'Detest' is a pretty strong word."

"And it fits."

Megan opened the door to the auditorium and led the way into the hushed room. "Without the kids, this place seems lifeless. I never get used to that. The stairs to the stage are over there."

"When Ava had a role in the first-grade Martin Luther King assembly I sat in the middle row here," he said, following her up. Close enough that she felt his warmth, but not touching. She missed his guiding hand on her lower back, but no contact seemed best.

Standing center stage, he stared out at the empty chairs. "Are the kids seated by grade level?"

"Yes, with the youngest children in the front rows and the oldest in the rear. Would you like to go backstage?"

"Nah, I'm good."

"Then I'll walk you out."

This time Max led the way down the stairs and through the auditorium.

"May your winning streak continue," Megan said at the school entrance.

"It will if I can help it. Enjoy dinner at your mom's."

In her room, Megan collected her purse and school papers, and gave herself props for a job well done.

She'd kept her feelings in check and had focused on the assembly. Max had responded in kind.

She ought to be sagging in relief. Then why did she feel so disappointed?

MEGAN'S STEPFATHER, Bennett, opened the door with a warm smile. "Come on in, honey."

Tall with thinning hair, he bent his head and tapped his cheek for a kiss. Over the years, Megan had grown to love him.

Her mother bustled in from the kitchen. Hugs and more cheek kisses followed. "I'm glad you're here," she said. "It seems like forever since we've seen you."

"Sorry—I've been really busy. Something smells wonderful."

"Lasagna. No one makes it like your mother." Her stepfather licked his lips and her mother beamed.

"Wine?" he asked, leading the way to the kitchen.

"Yes, please."

In the narrow kitchen, Bennett and her mother wove around each other with practiced ease, one getting the wine, the other the snacks. After some seventeen years of marriage they seemed as comfortable together as a pair of worn slippers.

Megan wanted that someday. The trouble was, she wanted it with Max. Which could never be. And she was not going to think about him, at least not while she was here. She loaded the drinks and snacks on a tray and toted them to the living room, where a crackling fire waited.

"How's the online dating?" her mother asked.

"I'm doing it."

Her parents exchanged looks, and Bennett clucked his tongue. "Not going so well, huh?"

"You can't even imagine."

Her mother patted her hand. "Don't give up."

"I won't." It'd help if she met a man as amazing as Max... Heck, she'd settle for half as amazing. Jeesh. Determined to steer away from men and dating, she changed the subject. "It's been quite a week at Guff's Lake School."

Her mother's eyes lit up. Having retired from teaching high school some two years earlier, she enjoyed hearing about Megan's experiences. "Tell me about it."

"This year's flu is in full swing. Some kids are out for eight or nine days, which makes learning difficult. I don't want anyone to fall behind."

"Of course not. How are you handling that?"

"If a student misses more than two days I email parents for updates. If they feel their son or daughter will be out more than four days, I forward the lessons we've covered in class and any homework."

Her mother nodded. "Thank goodness for email. I ran into Betty Randall the other day."

One of the biggest gossips in town. Megan rubbed her hands together. "I can't wait to hear the latest juicy story."

"This one happens to be about you."

"Me?" Megan couldn't imagine. "Except a few bad dates, I haven't done anything worth mentioning."

"Not according to Betty. She saw you at Bigelow's last weekend with one of the firefighters from the benefits calendar."

Oh, dear God. The woman sure got around. Megan stifled a groan. "I did run into Max Meier, Mr. June, there. We talked a bit—that's all."

Never mind what happened later.

"Still, it's interesting," her mother said. "I wasn't aware you knew any firefighters personally."

"Don't go getting any ideas, Mom. I met Max when his niece, Ava, brought him to school for Career Day a few weeks ago."

"What a clever way to meet someone. Why aren't you seeing him? Surely he's attracted to you. No man in his right mind wouldn't be. Unless he has a girlfriend or is married."

"I'm your daughter. You're slightly biased. But yes, he's single."

"Then why aren't you dating him?"

"Because sometime in the near future I want to get married. Max doesn't. When will dinner be ready?"

"In about fifteen minutes. About you and Max..."

"There is no Max and me. Be sure and tell Betty. I don't want to talk about him anymore."

Her mother sighed. "All right. Did you meet any other single men at Career Day?"

"I wouldn't know—I don't go around asking my students' fathers about their marital status."

"You don't have to get snippy about it."

"Sorry. It's a sensitive subject." Megan smiled to show that all was well. "Why don't I toss the salad and set the table?"

"Great. I'll take the foil off the lasagna and let it brown."

"I'll be in to help shortly," Bennett said and headed for the powder room.

Megan's mother linked arms with her. "When I taught I always enjoyed finding out what people did for a living."

Megan agreed. "It's fun to learn about different careers."

Her mother eyed her. "All of a sudden you look sad. Have you been thinking about your father lately?"

The perceptive question caught Megan by surprise. She had been. "Yes, I think because Ava, the girl I mentioned, and I have that in common.

Although she lost her father at a much younger age than I was when we lost Dad."

The rest of the evening passed uneventfully. Megan left with a container of leftovers, a slight headache, and the urge to binge on ice cream.

13

"Thanks for helping me out," Max's sister said when he showed up to watch Ava Thursday afternoon. His niece had been sick for days. "My boss has been great about letting me work from home this week, but the meeting this afternoon is important—even if I am the lowly bookkeeper in the back room. I'll be home as soon as I can."

"No rush. Is Ava in bed?"

Helen nodded. "Fast asleep."

"That's good. She needs rest to whip that flu bug. It sure is hanging on."

"For too long. I'm beginning to worry."

"She'll be all right," Max assured her. "But it can't hurt to take her to the doctor."

"The nurse said the same thing when I called earlier. We have an appointment tomorrow."

Max helped Helen into her coat. "Do I need to give her medicine or anything else?"

"Cough syrup if she needs it, and food and

liquids. There's chicken noodle soup in the fridge and ginger ale in the pantry, but you may have to coax her. She hasn't been hungry."

"I'll do my best. Too bad she won't make the assembly tomorrow. I kinda wanted to show off and make her proud."

"She's already proud of you and so am I."

Max gave a modest shrug, but he could hear that every day.

Her hand on the door, Helen paused. "By the way, Megan called this morning to check on Ava. They spoke for a few minutes. Ava was smiling when she hung up. That's one special teacher."

Didn't he know it. He wouldn't touch her again. But God above, he wanted to...

Erotic images crowded his mind—Megan flushed and restless, her legs around his hips... He started to get worked up and quickly banished the images.

The assembly couldn't be over soon enough. At least he'd be too busy talking about safety to think about sex.

Helen frowned. "You have the strangest look on your face, like you're starving and there's nothing to eat. Help yourself to anything in the fridge."

"Will do." His hunger had nothing to do with food. He blanked his expression. "Megan's good people."

"Ava's best teacher yet. I left half a pot of coffee from this morning for you, and if you're in the mood for sweets, there are cookies and granola ba—" Helen broke off. "Are you even listening?"

Kind of difficult with his one-track mind on Megan. "Coffee, cookies, and granola bars," he repeated.

"You did hear me. Still, you seem distracted. You have been since I mentioned Megan." Helen gave him a speculative look. "If you're interested in her, I approve."

"Don't you have a meeting to get to?"

"I can stay a few more minutes."

Her fists settled on her hips, the same as when she'd been eleven and forced into mothering his nine-year-old ass, their parents too mired in grief over the loss of Janet to pay them much attention.

No point in trying to outwit his sister. "Megan and I are a bad fit," he explained. "We want different things."

"How can you possibly know that?"

"Not that it's any of your business, but we talked about it."

"And when was this?"

"Butt out."

"Fine, don't answer. You'd better treat Megan nice. She's important to Ava and to me."

Helen left, her warning hanging in the air.

"Nice" didn't even skim the surface of what Max wanted with Megan. Try deep and hot...

And there went his mind again. His body also got in on the action, and he started to get hard.

Muttering, he headed down the hall and peeked in on Ava. Surrounded by her favorite "stuffies"—her word for stuffed animals—she was out cold. She looked so little and still.

As still as Janet had in the hospital...

With ruthless determination he cut off the macabre memory—but not the chill shuddering through him.

What the hell? She'd died a long time ago. Anyway, Ava hadn't been on a bike since last fall and she always wore a helmet. She had the flu and would be well in no time.

All the same, Max was shaken. He returned to the kitchen, nuked a mug of coffee, and promptly burned the shit out of his mouth.

As bad as it hurt, he welcomed the distraction from his black thoughts.

"WE TALKED ABOUT FIRE SAFETY, equipment, and what to do if a fire starts where you are," Max summarized as the assembly wound down. "I shared stories of some of our most unusual rescues and answered your questions. We're almost out of time, so let's get to that contest. Unless you'd rather skip it."

"No!" the kids shouted.

He'd expected that and smiled. "At the start of the assembly I asked you to guess the weight of all this gear I wear, including my air pack, thermal imaging camera, radio, box light, and axe. You wrote your guess on slips of paper and your teachers averaged the numbers. They handed the results to Principal Herman. She'll take it from here."

Kids sat forward, even the eighth-graders excited as the well-dressed, middle-aged principal joined Max on stage. "The correct weight is seventy-five pounds," she said. "Congratulations, students in Mr. Johnson's seventh-grade class for the closest guess of seventy-seven pounds. You win a tour of the Guff's Lake Fire Department."

The kids in the winning class whistled and smiled before she silenced them. "Thank you for a valuable and outstanding program, Mr. Meier," she added.

Everyone applauded. And that was that, the assembly was over.

The principal piled on the platitudes, calling the program "valuable and outstanding." He acknowledged the enthusiastic applause with a dip of his head.

The end of the school day was fast approaching, and everyone stood and began filing out to get ready to leave.

"You did an exceptional job," Principal Herman said to him. "We'd like to thank you with this." She attempted to hand him a check.

Max shook his head. "Due to city and state regs, I can't accept payment."

"But the amount has been recorded in our budget." She looked thoughtful. "What if we donate it to the benefit fund?"

"That you can do. Thanks."

As soon as he packed his equipment and descended from the stage kids surrounded him. He set his things aside and talked with several before Megan and her third-graders wandered over.

"I have to get my students back to the classroom and out the door, but we wanted to thank you for a great assembly," she said. "We all learned a lot."

He grinned. "I like that. A couple of seventh- and eighth-graders asked about getting jobs at the station."

"I'm not at all surprised. What did you tell them?"

"That when they're eighteen they can volunteer at the station, and to come see us after they get a college degree and earn a paramedic certification."

"A plug for college—great. I'm sorry Ava missed this. When we spoke on the phone yesterday I could tell she wanted to be here."

The mere mention of his niece's name brought back the irrational fears that had dogged him since the day before.

Megan frowned. "Is she worse?"

Realizing he'd clenched his jaw, Max forced

himself to relax. "I don't know. Helen took her to the doctor today."

"I think I would, too. Ava isn't the only child missing school. This is a particularly nasty strain of the flu, and some of our students are out for weeks. One fifth-grader was absent almost a month. I'm sure Ava will get well soon."

"So I keep telling myself." His collar, unbuttoned at the neck, felt too tight. He tugged at it.

Her eyes were twin pools of concern. "Hold on while I ask Ingrid to walk my students back." She signaled her friend, then returned her attention to Max. "You're really worried."

A lot more than made sense. "Seeing my normally energetic niece lying listless in bed..." He considered mentioning Janet but saw no point when it wasn't relevant. "It's rough."

Megan's understanding nod and open expression let him know she was there for him.

He grasped hold of that like a lifeline. He needed her warmth and light and the distraction she was sure to provide from his dismal thoughts. "Can I see you tonight?"

She hesitated, her internal struggle as clear as any words. Spending time with him wouldn't help her reach her goals for the future.

He shifted his weight. "Yeah, it's probably a bad idea. Forget I asked."

"I can't do that, Max. You need a friend and I want to help."

"Is that what we are—friends?"

She gave him a long look. "Today we are. I should get back to my students, but I'll meet you later. Tell me where and when."

He didn't want to be around other people. "Your place. I'll bring food."

"As long as you don't mind a mess. I haven't cleaned in a while."

"That won't bother me. What do you want to eat?"

"I haven't had a cheeseburger and fries in a while."

"Burgers and fries it is. What time?"

"An hour and a quarter?"

"See you then."

14

As soon as Megan walked in the door Bling meowed and twined himself around her ankles. "I missed you, too, but Max will be here soon and this place is a disaster. Your dinner will have to wait."

This afternoon she'd glimpsed something in him she hadn't before—genuine fear for his niece's welfare.

The cat stared up at her with eyes that didn't understand, and as she exchanged her school clothes for jeans and a pullover sweater she felt compelled to explain. "Max needs someone to keep him company, and out of all the single women he could spend the evening with, he chose me." She couldn't not be there for him. "Don't worry, I have no illusions about a future with him. This is a one-time thing, I swear."

Surely for a few hours she could set her growing feelings for him aside and be the friend he seemed to need so badly. Regardless, she preferred to show him into a tidy house.

Rushing around like a woman struck mad, she emptied the trash, loaded the breakfast dishes into the dishwasher, shoved the papers that mysteriously seemed to multiply during the night into drawers, and otherwise straightened up.

By now it was nearly dark outside and she stopped to flip on the porch light.

Bling grew more anxious by the second. Not wanting to take the time to feed him his usual canned food, she threw a handful of kibble into his bowl. "Snack on that while I vacuum the living room. Then I promise I'll feed you."

PARKED across the street from Megan's townhouse, Max sat in the Explorer and wondered why he was here. She'd left the drapes open and light blazed through the windows, a welcoming beacon in the darkness. Unable to tear his gaze away he watched her vacuum the living room, which for some reason soothed him.

Weird, but whatever worked. He felt battered, as if a bandage had been ripped from a wound not yet healed, and he needed all the help he could get.

Taking the food from the passenger seat he

exited the car. Moments later, slightly winded, Megan let him in.

"You didn't need to vacuum for me," he said.

"You saw that?"

"Me and anyone bothering to look." He nodded at the window. "Your curtains are wide open."

Laughing, she pulled them shut. "I've been too busy cleaning to realize."

"Like I said, I wouldn't have noticed." He glanced around and saw no sign of the mess she'd mentioned. "The place looks fine."

"As long as you don't look in any drawers or the coat closet."

Already in better spirits, he grinned. "I'll leave my jacket on the bench like last time." He handed her the food and shrugged out of his coat.

"Oh, this smells good." She peered into the bag.

"Hungry?"

"Starving. So is Bling."

Bending down, Max greeted the mewling cat. "Hey, big guy. You're not happy at all."

"He gets this way around mealtime. It stems from when he was a stray, never getting enough to eat. As soon as I got home I fed him a snack but it wasn't enough. Time for dinner, Bling."

Max followed her into the kitchen and sat at the eating bar while she took care of the tom. As soon as she set Bling's bowl on the floor he calmed right down. Just as Max had around her.

"Now it's our turn." Megan nodded at a bottle on the counter. "On winter evenings I usually unwind with a glass of wine."

"What about summers?" he asked.

"There's no school—I'm pretty much unwound all the time."

For the first time in days, he chuckled.

"I didn't have time to buy beer, but if you'd rather have water or milk..." she offered.

"Wine sounds good."

While he freed the cork from the bottle, Megan set plates, napkins, and glasses on the bar. Then she joined him. They dug in and finished the meal fast. Cleanup was a snap.

"If I weren't here, what would you be doing tonight?" he asked.

"Watching TV."

"Anything special?"

"The most recent episode of This Is Us. I recorded it last night."

"I like that show. I'll watch with you."

"Okay. I'll bring the glasses, you take the bottle."

They headed for the living room. When Max had last been here, he hadn't noticed much about the room. He did now. Three pale blue walls, the one with the gas fireplace a deep red. The furniture looked comfy and friendly, just like her. She started the fire and they plunked themselves on the couch facing the TV.

"This is cozy," he said.

"My little oasis of peace and harmony."

Exactly what Max needed. Too bad he couldn't soak up both by sitting here. He poured refills. Megan frowned and he realized he was holding the bottle in a death grip.

"You're so tense my own stomach has knots," she said. "Any word from Helen?"

Max shook his head. As bad as he wanted an update, he'd decided against contacting her.

"No news is a good sign, right?"

"Yeah." Maybe. If not... Tasting bile, he drained his wine. He set the empty glass on the coffee table.

She did the same. "Why don't you do yourself a favor and call her?"

Too scared. "She's got her hands full. I'll wait until morning. I thought you wanted to watch your show."

"Another time." Megan kicked off her shoes and turned to face him, crossing her legs on the cushion. "Talk to me, Max."

"This flu thing with Ava has done a number on me. I keep thinking about Janet—my little sister."

Damn, he hadn't meant to bring that up. He was here to forget, to shove the bad stuff back where it belonged, buried in the past. He waved his hand. "It's not important."

"Apparently it is. I'd like to hear about her."

Her caring tone and complete attention pulled the words out of him. "Even though Janet was younger than me, we palled around a lot. My parents said she worshipped me. I don't know about that, but I liked teaching her stuff."

Megan nodded. "I see that all the time at school."

"It happened in summer when Helen and I were both at day camp. Janet was too little and stayed home."

Remembering hurt. He refilled his glass after all and drained it. "I was in the shower after a swim in Guff's Lake when a counselor called me aside. He said Janet had been in an accident. A neighbor picked Helen and me up and drove us to the hospital."

Images sharp as broken glass cut through Max's mind, as clear as if they'd happened yesterday. His sister, motionless and white, hooked up to beeping machines while doctors and nurses conferred in low voices. His parents, broken by fear and sorrow. Him and Helen, crying and clinging to each other.

"I told you before that Janet had been riding her bike around the neighborhood without her helmet. We never found out why she wasn't wearing it. She never woke up." His voice hoarse from the strain of remembering and talking about it, he finished. "Three days later, she died."

"I'm so sorry," Megan said. A pause, and then... "Are you worried you might...might lose Ava?"

And he'd thought she was easy to read. He swallowed thickly.

Eyes filling, she peeled his fingers from the stem of his glass and set it down.

Aw damn, please don't cry. If she did, he might.

Fighting for control he squeezed the bridge of his nose. "I hate to see any kid in distress. But Ava... If anything happens to her..." He choked back an anguished howl.

"Don't go there, Max."

She wrapped her arms around him, her silent solace a balm to his despairing soul. Absorbing her giving warmth, he hugged her back.

Moments later the pain gave way to a voracious hunger for her. Not about to let go of her, he held her with one hand and tipped up her chin with the other. "I want you, Megan. Can I stay with you tonight?"

"Whatever you need."

"I need to lose myself in you."

"Then kiss me."

Holding back nothing, he devoured her mouth. She responded with equal passion, a glimpse of the pleasure waiting for him.

Somehow he tore his mouth away. "No promises, okay?"

"No expectations at all. I'm on the pill and I'm clean. Are you?"

"Yeah. You're positive you want to do this?"

In answer, she rose and took his hand.

15

Holding tight to Max on the way upstairs, Megan pushed any thoughts of the future from her mind. All that mattered was now and being with him. She'd wanted this since the evening at Lucky Joe's, and his need tonight only increased her desire.

They didn't get far before he pulled her into a searing kiss. When he released her they were both breathing hard.

Seizing her hand, he almost sprinted up the stairs. At the top he paused. "Which is your bedroom?"

"Second door on the left."

Moments later he tugged her inside. She flipped on the light and winced. Her shoes sat helter-skelter in the middle of the rug and her dress and tights lay where she'd tossed them on the unmade bed. If she'd had any inkling this would happen, she'd have straightened up. Too late now.

Max didn't seem to care. Sidestepping the shoes he hauled her up close. His passionate kiss hummed through all her body parts. Before long, her pullover and his T-shirt had disappeared.

Why had she worn a plain beige bra? The thought vanished under his warm look and his most excellent torso. Big-boned and pure muscle, courtesy of the intense physical training he put himself through.

And all hers—for tonight, anyway.

She ran her finger down his impressive abs, pleased when he sucked in an audible breath. She'd dreamed of this, but reality was far better than any fantasy. "You actually have a six-pack," she commented in wonder.

"Keeping fit is part of the job."

"I approve."

He flashed a slow, sexy grin. "Your turn."

Reaching behind, she unfastened her bra and let it fall away. His growl of approval sharpened her nipples before he laid a finger on her.

Then...

He touched her.

Her low moan didn't begin to express the pleasure rippling through her whole body, turning her into a boneless, restless wreck. She needed to sit down, but Max hauled her close for a probing, possessive kiss.

Mouth open and demanding. Hard, hot body in her arms.

Her knees buckled.

He let out a low laugh, his strong arms holding her upright. "Someone needs to lie down."

Megan flung her school clothes and the blanket aside. On the bed, she lost herself in sensation. In Max. His unique scent. His lips teasing down her neck, collarbone, and breasts.

Bliss... Only not quite.

She wanted him between her legs. Now. Impatient, she reached for his fly.

"Easy." He lifted her hand, turned it over, and planted a tender kiss where her wrist met her palm.

"That does not make me want to slow down. I need you, Max."

"I can't do anything while you're wearing those jeans. Lift up."

She raised her hips. Her jeans and panties disappeared. Naked, she lay before him.

Heat turned his whiskey brown eyes to burnished gold. "God above, you're beautiful."

Kneeling between her legs, he did something amazing with his tongue and fingers.

Yes!

Seconds later, wet and wild for more, she arched up and gasped. "I'm about to come."

"Go for it." He went back to what he was doing.

She orgasmed hard. When she finally returned to sanity, Max kissed her.

One kiss turned into another. Before long, she

wanted him again. Desperately. She wrapped her legs around him. "This time I need you inside me."

"Exactly where I want to be."

One thrust and he was buried deep. He knew how to move and stimulate. Another climax built. As she began to spin out of control, he joined her. The world splintered into a rainbow of color.

After, she lay spent beside him. Sex had never been like this. She felt joyful and content, satisfied clear to her toes.

Complete.

Max kissed her gently. "How are you feeling?"

Leaning on his chest, she beamed at him. "Pretty darned spectacular."

"Yeah?" A satisfied grin lit his face.

"I think you're all better, too," she teased.

"And then some."

He tucked her close to his side and nuzzled the crook of her shoulder. With a plaintive meow, Bling jumped on the bed. Max shook his head and chuckled. "Good thing he didn't try that while we were making love. Keep her company for me, big guy. I'll be right back."

Gloriously naked he padded from the room without any of the self-consciousness Megan would have felt.

What a guy. Smiling, she hugged herself. Life would be perfect if only he wanted a real relationship...

She quickly shut down the thought. She

knew the risks, but he needed her tonight and she didn't regret one second of what they'd shared. The sorrow he harbored over the loss of his sister made her ache for him, both for the boy he'd been and the man he was now. Helping him forget his troubles for a few hours was her gift to him, and she'd happily do it again without thinking twice. All night long, if Max wanted.

Megan certainly did. In the heat of passion she didn't think about the future, only the man in her arms. Tonight was all that mattered.

Except for one little catch. As she'd known all along, sex had complicated matters. She was dangerously close to falling in love with Max.

Close to falling in love? The truth was, she'd fallen for him before he'd even kissed her tonight. From the moment the haunted look had crossed his face in the auditorium and he'd voiced his fears for Ava, he'd owned her heart.

Megan had no idea what to do about that.

ON HIS WAY out of the bathroom, Max grinned. Sex with Megan—phenomenal. Out of bed she rocked his world in a different way, listening while he talked about the past and opening her arms to him.

How had she known he'd needed that?

She grounded him and asked for nothing in

return, and his gratitude almost brought him to his knees. He'd never met a woman like her.

He wasn't sure what to make of the feelings crowding his chest and wasn't inclined to dwell on them. All he knew was, the night was young and he wanted more.

The thick carpet masked his footsteps and Megan didn't hear him return. Taking advantage of the moment, he paused in the shadows outside the bedroom and studied her.

He expected to see a satisfied smile on her face, not a wrinkled brow. She looked unhappy.

What was that about?

His empty belly growled and her startled gaze flew to him. "Listen to you."

"I'm hungry again."

The corners of her mouth tilted upward, which was more like it. "Me, too, and it hasn't been that long since dinner."

"Great sex will do that. Got anything good in the fridge?"

"Tons." She sat up, taking the blanket with her. "What are you in the mood for?"

"You for dessert. For the main course, I make a mean grilled cheese sandwich."

"Yum. I happen to have a can of tomato soup to go with it."

"Come on, then." He tossed her his shirt, then stepped commando into his jeans.

While they cooked and ate he teased her. She

laughed and teased back. No sign of that frown now.

As soon as they cleaned up the food mess, he reached for her. "I need something sweet to cap off the meal."

On the way to the bedroom, she wrapped her thighs around his hips. They never made it past the living room. He loved her on the rug in the glow of the fire.

Sometime later, sated after red-hot shower sex, he wrapped her in a towel and carried her to bed. As he set her down he heard his cell phone ring. He'd left it in his jacket pocket.

"That could be Helen," he said. Although it was after ten, and she never called this late.

Senses alert, he strode down the hall and snatched up the phone. Yep, it was Helen. He answered on the way back to the bedroom. "Hey there. What'd the doctor say?"

When she told him, he swore softly. "Be there in twenty."

Megan had lost her drowsy, satisfied expression and was tying the sash of her robe around her waist. "What did she say, Max?"

He filled her in while he dressed. "Ava doesn't have the flu. Earlier today her pediatrician ordered blood tests for various illnesses. He just called Helen with the results. All tests came back negative. He thinks Ava could have leukemia."

Megan covered her mouth with her fingers. "How does a person get that?"

"Hell if I know. The doctor scheduled her to meet with a pediatric oncologist in Portland tomorrow for a consultation and more tests. Children's Hospital is preparing a room for her now. Helen wants to get there stat. I'm driving."

Her expression troubled, Megan clasped his hands. "What can I do, Max?"

"Pray." His voice broke.

He hugged her hard, then raced for his car.

16

Max had been on the road less than ten minutes before Ava fell asleep. He and Helen had buckled her into the back seat with a pillow, blanket, and her favorite stuffies for comfort.

Helen yawned. She was exhausted. "You need rest," he said. "Get it while you can."

"I don't dare close my eyes. Every time I do... You don't want to know." She rubbed her arms as if chilled to the marrow. "I called you twice tonight before you picked up. Where were you?"

"At Megan's." Lost in the wonder of her heat and softness.

"Finally some good news. I knew you liked her. I'm happy for you both."

His sister's smile was a welcome relief, but Max didn't want her getting the wrong idea. "I wouldn't go that far. Megan's great but we aren't officially seeing each other. I'm not sure what we're doing."

"Is she aware of that?"

"Like I said the other day, she knows how I feel about serious relationships and marriage."

"And you think she believes you?"

"Why wouldn't she? I've been straight with her from the get-go."

His sister's laugh lacked any humor. "You're so clueless, but all men are." A moment later she gave him a dirty look. "Megan means a lot to Ava and me. Promise me you won't break her heart."

Causing her pain was the last thing he wanted. "You have to ask?"

"Did you sleep with her?"

He snorted. "What kind of question is that?"

"You did. I swear to God, Max, if you hurt her I will wring your neck."

With more than four inches of height and sixty-odd pounds on her, not likely. Still, when she used that mothering tone, he felt like a little kid again.

He narrowed his eyes. "Lay off."

"Fine, but consider yourself warned." Helen clamped her lips together and showed him her back. Before long the tension drained from her body. She'd fallen asleep.

At this hour there were few cars on the road, and after Max crossed the mountain passes, which could be treacherous in winter, he played the radio low and let his mind drift. Except to Ava's illness. He couldn't go there and drive safely.

He reviewed recent emergency calls and training sessions with teammates, then moved on to woodworking projects. The headboard for Adam and Sam, Ava's jewelry box, an order from a new customer for a custom coffee table, and what to do with a slab of walnut sitting in his workshop. No idea about the walnut.

The rest he hashed through pretty quick. Then he thought about Megan.

And agreed with Helen—she mattered. Once again his chest swelled with the feelings he'd dismissed at her place. Here in the car with little to distract him, his emotions weren't so easy to ignore. He still didn't fully understand them, only knew they scared him almost as much as Ava's illness. Go figure.

His head began to pound. His shoulders were all knotted up and his hands ached, likely from clenching the wheel. He loosened his fingers, rolled his shoulders, massaged his temples. And decided he'd best not think about Megan right now.

He devoted the last hour of the drive to the upcoming in-house training sessions he'd scheduled. He needed to nudge Captain Comings to write that recommendation and forward it to the community college.

When he finally pulled into the hospital parking area, he exhaled in relief.

~

HER MIND on Max and his family, Megan tossed and turned half the night. In the best of weather conditions, the drive to Portland took three hours. Crossing the icy mountain passes in the dark of night would take longer.

Had they arrived safe and sound, and what would the experts at Children's Hospital find when they examined Ava?

With such worrisome questions running through Megan's mind, how could she possibly sleep? "Please, let Ava be all right," she murmured in a heartfelt prayer for the little girl, Max, and his entire family.

Needing comfort, she hugged the pillow that smelled of Max. His potent scent reminded her of the hours spent in his arms, his passion and tenderness... The sensitive places in her body throbbed with a different kind of tension.

Tonight she'd sensed a shift in him. Turning to her for solace, trusting her enough to let her see his pain, loving her with a passion she'd never experienced. He cared about her.

Maybe he'd change his mind and decide he wanted a future together...

Only he wouldn't. Hadn't he pulled back to remind her?

No promises, okay?

And no sense wasting time and energy aching for what would never be. At least he didn't know she loved him. If he had the vaguest idea, he'd freak out.

Megan was a little freaked herself. Now that Max owned her heart, finding her forever guy seemed daunting, almost impossible.

Instead of worrying about that she thought about his last, heartfelt hug and the painful crack in his voice. Love her or not, he still needed her.

She would be there for him, helping any way she could.

Consoled at last, she slept.

17

With a loud meow, Bling jumped on the bed and butted Megan's chin, a rude awakening. "All right, all right," she mumbled, rubbing sleep from her eyes.

Stumbling into the bathroom, she put on her robe, then padded downstairs to the kitchen. As she filled his bowl and made coffee, the events of the night before flooded back. Max opening up and the hours of wonderful sex brought to an abrupt end by Helen's phone call.

Weighted down by Ava's illness and doubt that her own future would include Max, Megan didn't want to be alone. After showering and dressing she sat down to breakfast and texted Ingrid. Need 2 come over asap.

To her relief the reply was immediate. Unlocking the door now.

Some twenty minutes later Ingrid ushered Megan into her kitchen, where the table was set with a steaming coffee pot, two mugs, a carton of milk, and a bowl of sugar. "Sit," she said, gesturing at a seat. "For you to be dressed and out this early on a Saturday... Let me guess—you need to talk about Max and last night."

Megan hung her coat on the back of her chair and helped herself to her second and much-needed coffee of the day. "How in the world did you guess?"

"Anyone with eyes saw the way you two looked at each other after the assembly. It was obvious where you were headed. Also, you have a love bite on your neck."

Megan touched the place where Max had marked her with his passion and made a mental note to wear a turtleneck Monday. No sense adding to the speculation among her peers.

"You're right—Max came over. He stayed for quite a while." Ingrid gave a knowing nod. "The worst has happened—I'm in love with him. Which he doesn't know and won't."

Her friend opened her mouth, no doubt to ask questions Megan didn't want to answer. She continued. "Something else had happened that concerns Ava. It's bad."

"Ava?" Ingrid gave a confused frown. "Has she developed complications from the flu?"

"She doesn't have the flu. Max's sister, Helen, took her to her pediatrician yesterday. He ran tests for other possible illnesses. They all came back negative. He thinks Ava might have leukemia."

Despite the warmth in the room, Megan felt chilled to the bone. She cupped the hot mug against her chest. Ingrid had gone motionless with shock.

"As soon as Max heard from Helen, he left to pick her and Ava up and drive them to Portland. Ava has a meeting with a specialist and will undergo more tests."

"Children's Hospital there is amazing," Ingrid said. "My friend's cousin had a brain tumor and went there for treatment. It's been four years and he's doing great."

"That's reassuring, but Ava doesn't have a brain tumor."

"And that's something to be grateful for. You said more tests, which means her pediatrician doesn't know for sure what's wrong with her. Maybe it isn't leukemia."

"One can hope." Megan crossed her fingers on both hands. "Whatever she has, this is serious."

"When do you think you'll hear from Max?"

"He didn't say."

Ingrid nodded. "Logan and I are supposed to hang out together this afternoon, but I'm happy to cancel and spend the day with you."

"You're a good friend, but someone should enjoy a normal Saturday. Besides, I need to hold and comfort a baby this afternoon. I think I'll go home now."

At the door, she and Ingrid clung to each

other. When they pulled back they both had tears in their eyes.

"The second you hear anything, call or text," Ingrid said. "Meantime, I'll send up a prayer."

LATE SATURDAY AFTERNOON Max sat in the hospital waiting room, wishing he could get into the thriller he'd bought at the gift shop. Too much on his mind.

The good news: Ava didn't have leukemia or cancer of any kind. The bad news: the doctors were stumped. Without a diagnosis they couldn't treat the mysterious disease. Treatment his gravely ill niece sorely needed.

Which was why the poor kid was being subjected to a battery of tests to determine the cause of her illness. While Helen stayed at her side, comforting her as only a mom could, the rest of the family had been banished to the waiting room.

Leaving Max with his parents, which was about as pleasant as a dislocated shoulder.

Seated with their current spouses on opposite sides of the low-slung table between them, they acted as if each other were invisible.

With Ava fighting for her life, Max had figured they'd put their differences aside and get along. Nope. He bit back the urge to chew them out. Why bother, when it wouldn't do any good?

Moments ago his father's wife and his mother's husband, who were more adult about the situation and almost cordial toward each other, had headed to the cafeteria for snacks. Leaving Max to bear the freeze fest alone.

Although his parents rarely glanced at each other, now and then their faces pinched in shared pain and fear. No doubt they recalled another dark time—the awful days leading up to Janet's death.

"Ask your mother if she has a clean tissue," his dad said, squinting at the screen of his laptop.

Max's mom, a long-time knitter, was working on something beige, her needles flying. The click-clack grew louder, signaling irritation. "Tell your father to use the TP in the men's room."

His father shot eye daggers at her.

Max lost his cool. "Both of you, stop it!"

His mother harrumphed and his father tightened his jaw, but neither softened.

At one time they'd been happy together. When they'd lost Janet everything had changed.

What would happen if Ava...

Max cut off the thought before it finished, but not soon enough. Agony rose up in his chest until he wanted to roar. He needed Megan so bad he'd trade ten years of his life to hold her for five minutes. Soaking up her warmth, accepting all the TLC she had to give.

Unable to sit one more second, he jumped up.

"I'm going to get some air. If anything happens, call."

He caught an elevator to the ground floor and exited the hospital. Bowing his head against the sleeting rain, hands shoved in his jacket pockets, he tromped around the perimeter of the building and headed for the coffee place he'd discovered earlier that morning.

As he crossed the street toward the pink and brown Buster's Café sign, a couple sharing an umbrella ambled toward him. Heads close together they spoke in low voices, lost in a world where only they existed.

Max envied them. And again wished Megan were here with him. He slid his phone from his pocket and started to call her.

What would he say? That the doctors didn't know anything yet and he needed to lose himself in her?

Megan cared about him. If he asked, she'd drive up. He couldn't do that, couldn't allow himself to get even more tangled up with her. Because face it, Helen was right—she could get hurt. God knew, he didn't want that on his head.

What in hell had possessed him, going to her place last night and making love a bunch of times, when he knew damn well she wanted a ring on her finger and children?

Not Max. He didn't want a family of his own, ever. Marriage didn't last, and kids... They had accidents or fell ill.

Sometimes they died.

Please, let the doctors figure this thing out. Let Ava make it.

Wretched and chilled clear to his bones he stopped smack in the middle of the crosswalk, put the cell phone away and accepted that as bad as he wanted to be with Megan, he wouldn't. He could never give her what she wanted. The price was too high.

A blaring horn startled him from his desolate thoughts. Shaking his head for stopping in the middle of the street—talk about dangerous—he jogged to the opposite sidewalk.

In the café he ordered an extra-large coffee, snagged a table, and sat down to drink it. After a few sips, he buried his face in his hands.

"You all right, buddy?" asked a kindly voice.

Heaving a weary breath, Max raised his head. Standing at his shoulder, a heavyset, grizzled man with a shaggy beard who had to be in his seventies regarded him with friendly concern.

"I'm okay," Max replied. Dangling by a thread.

"You must have a loved one in the hospital."

"My niece."

The man gave a solemn nod. "I'm Jasper." He dug into his shirt pocket and produced a worn business card. "I'm here every day, usually at that table by the window. If you ever want to talk, play a game of checkers, or sit silently with a friend..." He clapped Max's shoulder, then left him be.

Max nursed his coffee and returned to his

thoughts. At the very least he should let Megan know he'd arrived safely and explain about the tests. He also needed to tell her they couldn't be together again. But at the moment he was raw inside and in no shape even to text her, let alone have a conversation about Ava or their relationship.

What a piece of work he was.

I'll contact her soon. When he pulled himself together and manned up.

He checked his watch, then bussed his mug. Nodding at Jasper, he hunched his shoulders and headed outside, into the punishing rain.

18

Megan heard nothing from Max Saturday or Sunday. She didn't expect an hourly report, but an occasional update would have been nice. Was Ava better? What did her tests show? And what about Max—how was he? Not knowing was agony.

Several times she picked up her cell phone to contact him, but she didn't want to intrude.

By Sunday night she'd bitten her nails to the quick, a habit she'd given up in high school but resumed Friday night. Unable to bear Max's silence one more second, she called him. His phone went to voice mail, and Megan jumped to the worst possible conclusion—that Ava had grown even sicker.

Forget intruding, she needed information. Sucking in a calming breath, she did her best to mask her alarm. "Hi, Max, it's Megan. When you can, let me know how Ava is doing.

"Also, Principal Smith should know what's

happening. If you and Helen prefer, I'll update her for you. I need to know what to say. Please send my warmest regards to Helen and your family, and hug Ava for me."

Megan heard nothing that evening, but when the alarm woke her Monday morning she found a text from Max. At last.

Docs ruled out leukemia & other cancers. More tests but no answers yet. OK 2 share with principal. Helen thanks u. Got home late 2nite & working tomorrow. Heading back 2 Portland Wednesday. We'll talk later.

That was it. Megan didn't expect anything sexy or intimate, but a "miss you" or "I'll call when I can" would've been nice.

How selfish and petty was that? Here Max was, in the middle of a family crisis. He likely wasn't thinking about anything but Ava. On the other hand, he knew how worried Megan was. As soon as he found out Ava didn't have cancer, he should have told her.

Not bothering to hide her irritation, she replied. No cancer is good news. If you'd let me sooner, I'd still have fingernails.

Intent on getting his breakfast, Bling butted her shins and meowed with increasing force. "Stop it!" she snapped.

The cat shut up and blinked, his yellow eyes accusing. Instant contrition. None of this was his fault. "Sorry," she apologized. "I'll feed you right away."

At school, she told the principal and the staff about Ava. The news left everyone reeling with shock and worry. In the classroom, she explained that Ava was in the hospital, then gathered all her art supplies for a giant get-well card.

For the rest of the day she gave her all to her students, focusing on the here and now as a coping mechanism. On the outside she seemed calm and in control, but inside she was a tangled knot of anxiety.

"Any updates from Max?" Ingrid asked when she and Megan ambled through the parking lot that afternoon.

"Not since his text this morning. I'm sure he's busy fighting fires and keeping people safe."

"The guy sure doesn't contact you much."

Megan agreed. Max's communication skills needed serious work. "He'll get in touch when he can," she assured her friend.

But she was beginning to wonder.

THE CAPTAIN HAD GIVEN Max the okay to take sick leave and stay in Portland, but Max had declined. With Ava so sick his crewmates thought he was nuts for working.

"Waiting around in that hospital is torture," he explained over Monday morning breakfast. "I'd rather be here, working and doing good." Surrounded by the guys he trusted and loved like brothers, and too busy to stress over his niece or figure out how to tell Megan he couldn't see her again.

"My parents and stepparents are at the hospital with Ava and my sister," he added. "They'll keep me informed. I'll be back there Wednesday."

"That's good." Tony gave an approving nod.

Max bit into his breakfast sandwich.

Across the table, Hank scowled at him. "While you're gone, check in. You sure as hell didn't over the weekend."

Max eyed him. "There wasn't much to report."

"Your niece doesn't have leukemia and that's not news?"

He sounded a lot like Megan. Max wasn't about to admit that he hadn't been up to communicating with anyone. He'd felt too exposed. Still did.

Anyway, they all were up to date now.

"Even when there are no changes we need to know," Tony said. "Hell, if any of us stood in your shoes, you'd expect the same thing."

Max rolled his eyes, but the guy had a point.

The captain frowned and stood. "We care, Max. I'll see you all in ten."

After he left, the rest of the crew added their two cents.

"I assume you told Megan about Ava," Ethan said.

Max nodded. "I was with her when Helen phoned Friday night."

The smartass grinned. "Wondered why you were a no-show at the poker game. And you said you weren't getting involved with her."

"It's not like that," Max explained. Or wouldn't be, once he told her he couldn't see her again. A conversation he dreaded worse than sitting around the hospital. "After the assembly Friday afternoon we talked about Ava. We were both worried. That's how we ended up together."

Nate raised his eyebrows. "Define 'together.' "

Max's glare did nothing to erase his bud's knowing grin. To his relief the alarm on his phone chimed, signaling five minutes until the meeting.

His crewmates cleaned up their breakfast mess and split, Max hanging back to finish the last of his meal. But the comments about him and Megan had messed with his appetite, and he ended up tossing the remains.

He missed her like crazy, but tough beans. They needed to talk ASAP. Which meant by phone instead of in person. Tonight if possible, depending on emergency calls.

With that storm cloud hanging over him, he hastened down the stairs to the apparatus bay.

19

Megan was grading math homework Monday night when Max called. About darned time.

That wasn't fair. The man had spent an intense weekend in Portland and had been at work since eight a.m. this morning—more than twelve hours. Determined to be supportive she picked up with a smile in her voice. "Hi."

"Hey, Megan."

Hearing her name in his deep voice made her go soft inside. Oh, she had it bad. "How's your shift going?"

"Busy as always. If an emergency call comes in, I'll be hanging up fast."

"Do you get a lot of those at night?"

"Around here we never know. I should have called from Portland, but with everything so crazy..."

"I can't even imagine. Your family must be so relieved Ava doesn't have cancer. The entire faculty and student body of Guff's Lake School certainly is."

"That is good news. On the downside, the doctors can't treat an illness they haven't been able to diagnose."

"I never thought of that. With Ava's situation so up in the air, why did you come back?"

"For the routine."

"To keep you from losing your mind," she guessed.

"Exactly. How did you know?"

"I've been there. When my father passed away all those years ago, my mom and I sat around paralyzed and lost in grief. After a few days of that, she insisted we get back to our routines. Returning to school and being with my friends saved my sanity."

"Your mom is smart. My parents could take a few lessons from her."

"That's right, they still don't get along."

"They don't even speak to each other. Any communication is done through me or Helen. Drives me nuts."

"That's no fun."

"You have no idea. It's been this way since we lost my little sister."

"Are they both at the hospital?"

"Yep, and still giving each other the silent treatment."

"You and Helen don't need that, especially now."

"Nope. It'd be better if they all just went home. Hey, I have news. Helen just called. Earlier tonight she sat with Ava, chatting away to cheer her up. She was reminiscing about the trip they made to Fresno over winter break, when they visited Ava's great aunt. She's the only living relative from Ava's dad's side and getting up there in age. They try to see her once a year."

"That's sweet," Megan said, not at all sure what that had to do with anything.

"While Helen talked about the trip, Dr. Barandie, one of the docs involved with Ava's case, stopped in to see her. When he heard she'd been in Fresno, a light bulb went off in his head. He thinks she may have contracted something called valley fever. The blood test for that was done this evening. We'll have the results in the next few days."

Megan frowned. "I've never heard of valley fever."

"Me, either. According to Dr. Barandie it comes from a fungus natural to the San Joaquin Valley. It's not common in Oregon or most of the US and the symptoms are often similar to those of other diseases. That's why no one here thought of it. Spores from the fungus enter the body through the lungs. Plenty of people are exposed but never fall sick. But Ava did."

"You say she's been to Fresno before. Why did she get it this time, and why did it take so long for her to get sick?"

"Beats me. I was told symptoms can take weeks to develop."

"Is it contagious?" Megan asked. If so, the school and parents needed to be alerted post haste.

"No."

That was a relief. "Is it curable?"

"If caught early."

She swallowed. "Ava's been sick for a couple of weeks."

"One step at a time, Megan. First, we wait for the test results."

"Right."

"Don't say anything until we know for sure."

"I won't. I wish we were together right now. I'd wrap myself around you so tight..."

"I could use one of your healing hugs."

He considered her hugs healing? Soaking up the praise, Megan closed her eyes. "Just now your voice got low and intimate, like when we make love. I want you."

Max groaned. "Don't."

"You're right. When we can't be together, getting all worked up seems pointless."

She heard him shifting around. "Look, we need to talk."

"Isn't that what we're doing?"

"I mean about you and me. I wish we could do this face-to-face, but I'm heading back to Portland as soon as my shift ends Wednesday."

That sounded an awful lot like good-bye. And

so soon. Megan stiffened her spine. "Whatever it is, say it."

"I need to focus on Ava. Between her, my job, and my woodworking projects, I don't have time for anything else."

He meant for her.

After an uncomfortable silence, he cleared his throat. "I can't get involved with you, Megan."

She sat back. "Kinda late for that."

"My fault. I should have stayed away."

Shoulda, woulda, coulda. "But you didn't. You needed me, and I..." She'd welcomed the chance to fill that need despite knowing the consequences. "I gave you exactly what you wanted."

Slipping into her usual please-your-man role without a second thought. She ought to change her name to Megan the Needy.

"You wanted to be with me, too," Max said.

She couldn't argue with that or regret one second of what they'd shared. Knowing she'd helped him forget his troubles for a while had heightened her emotions and opened her heart.

The time had come to distance herself from all that. "Why bring this up again, Max? I'm well aware of what you do and don't want, and I'm fine with it."

A blatant lie, but for the sake of her pride, necessary.

There are more fish in the sea. Funny how she latched onto that when she knew better.

"I'm relieved to hear that," he said. "Being with

you was amazing, and I'll never forget that. But it can't happen again."

Her mind had gone blank. Mute, she stared at the black pen she used on the math homework.

"This has nothing to do with you, it's on me," he added. "I'm sorry if I hurt you."

The last thing she wanted was his pity. "We had an evening together that we both enjoyed, period."

As she congratulated herself on her carefree tone, tears gathered behind her eyes. "I have papers to grade. I should go."

"I'll keep you posted about Ava."

"Please do."

Megan disconnected. Then she cried.

Taking a break from the hospital Thursday afternoon, Max wandered into Buster's Café. Stopping in for coffee once or twice a day had become a habit.

At only an hour or so before dinner, the place was almost empty, but Jasper was at his usual table with his checkerboard, mug, and a book. As always, he nodded.

Max returned the nod, got his coffee and sat down. Back home the Guff's Lake School day was about to end. He'd wait awhile before he contacted Megan and shared the latest from Dr. Barandie.

Great news that would make her happy. Hell, Max and his whole family were.

He also felt like he'd collided with a fast curveball—bruised and sore and plain lousy for breaking up with Megan. Small price to pay for putting a halt to their relationship before it went too far.

He wasn't the only one hurting. For all Megan's talk the other night, she couldn't hide her pain from him. Feeling worse than ever, he swore under his breath. As he nursed his coffee, he texted updates to the captain and his crewmates.

Then there was no more putting it off. Time to update Megan.

Not wanting Jasper or anyone else privy to whatever unfolded during the conversation, he put on his coat and left. At a city park nearby he found an empty bench. The seat was cold, but at least the frigid weather kept others away.

Her phone rang and rang before she picked up. "Hi, Max," she answered, sounding winded.

"You're out of breath."

"I was across the hall waiting for Ingrid to finish straightening up her classroom when I heard my phone."

She sounded friendly enough, but cool. He missed that special warmth that salved his soul.

Can't have it both ways, man. "If you're busy, phone me back later."

"Now is okay, but hold on." Although she covered the phone with her hand, he heard her. "Ingrid, I need to take this call. I'll see you tomorrow. All right, Max, I'm back. You must have news about Ava."

"Yep, and it's all good. Dr. Barandie was right —she has valley fever."

"Thank God, a diagnosis at last."

Max heard tears of relief in her voice and his own eyes watered.

Megan sniffled. "What happens now?"

"She's starting treatment as we speak. If all goes well, before long she'll be back to her normal self."

"That's wonderful. When does she get to come home?"

"We're not sure yet. There are side effects from the meds and the staff here need to monitor her for a while." Hating that his niece had to deal with side effects when she was already so ill, Max scrubbed the back of his neck. "Depending on how she responds, she'll be here anywhere from another week to several more."

"The important thing is that she gets well."

"Amen." Having accomplished the purpose of his call, he could hang up. But he wasn't quite ready. "How are you?"

"I'm doing fine, especially after such great news. Ava's classmates made her a get-well card even bigger than the thank-you card they made for you."

Max still had that card. "Nice—she'll like that."

"If she's up for visitors, I'd like to bring it to her, along with some homework, in case she doesn't have access to a laptop. I don't want her to fall too far behind."

"Her energy level seems to go up and down, and I can't speak for a visit. Check with Helen. The drive from Guff's Lake to Portland is a long one, especially over the passes in winter. I'd hate for you to spend all that time and effort getting here when she might not feel up to seeing you. You're welcome to leave the card and homework at the station's front desk. When I come back next week I'll bring it to her."

"I appreciate that, but I want to come up. If she can't see me, at least she'll know I made the attempt. Next week is midwinter break. We have Monday through Wednesday off. I'd like to come up Tuesday."

Max would be in Guff's Lake, working. He wouldn't run into her at the hospital, a big relief. So why did he feel the opposite? "I'll ask Helen to call you," he said.

"Okay, and thanks for the call. I'll share the good news with my principal and associates."

Professional and composed, she could have been talking to anyone. He winced. "Great."

"Take care."

He stared at the blank screen of his phone for

a long time before he stood and returned to the hospital.

20

Megan had lied to Max. Instead of doing well she was a pitiful mess. Saturday morning, wallowing in the depths of a poor me marathon, she moped around in her PJs. For breakfast, she polished off a half-gallon of chocolate ice cream. Which helped, but wasn't enough to drown out the ache inside. In need of something else to binge on, she rooted around in the pantry. She heard a knock at the door. Not wanting anyone to see her like this, she froze.

Another more insistent knock followed. "Megan, it's your mother. Open up."

Less than an hour ago they'd touched base by phone. What was she doing here?

"It's freezing outside. Let me in. I have goodies," her mother wheedled.

An offer Megan couldn't refuse. She smoothed her hair, a useless effort, and opened the door. "I'm not even dressed yet, and we already spoke. Is something wrong?"

"Not with me." Her mother bustled in, her gaze traveling from Megan's tangled hair to her bare feet. "I knew it! You're down in the dumps. This should cheer you up." She set a Samantha's Treats bakery bag on the eating bar. "Freshly baked scones, still warm from the oven."

Megan's mouth watered. "I've been craving a scone all morning. How did you guess?"

"I'm your mother—I have a sixth sense about these things. Do you have any coffee?"

Megan nodded and fixed her a mug. They sat down with the bakery bag between them. Some minutes later, Megan licked the last of a raspberry scone from her lips. "That helps a lot."

"I had a hunch it would. It's almost eleven a.m. and you haven't even showered. Something tells me this is about a man. Someone you've been dating?"

Sometimes her mom was too smart. Megan hadn't said a word about Max or that she'd deleted her profile from In the Cards. She didn't really want to talk about that, but her mother's arched eyebrows couldn't be ignored. She expected answers.

"All right, I'll tell you," Megan said. "I am feeling pretty bad about a guy. No one from the online dating scene, I'm taking a break from that. Remember when Betty Randall told you she saw me with Max and I explained why we weren't dating?"

"You want to get married and Max doesn't."

Megan gave a miserable nod. Admitting the rest was embarrassing but she plunged ahead. "We started dating anyway, which I saw no point in mentioning unless something good came from it." Avoiding her mother's assessing gaze, she fiddled with her paper napkin. "Nothing did."

She'd had a night of great sex and had fallen in love with him, but that was bad, not good.

All her talk about staying away from Max and focusing on finding her forever guy had been just that—talk. In the end, her main concern had been to be there for him, to please him. And yes, maybe hold his interest that way.

The same old, same old, and it was time to face the truth. Like it or not, no matter how hard she fought to change, at heart she was and forever would be pathetically eager to please.

"Oh, honey, I'm sorry."

Bristling at the pity emanating from her mother, Megan straightened her spine. "No one forced me to get involved with him. Even he reminded me multiple times that he didn't want a real relationship. I should have steered clear, but I didn't."

She hadn't been able to stop herself.

This time her mother remained silent, and Megan went on. "And Ava, his niece who's in my class, is seriously ill. He's wrapped up in her, as he should be. He doesn't want to see me anymore."

"Will Ava be all right?"

"The doctors think so, but for now, she's in the hospital in Portland. I'm planning to drive up and see her Tuesday, during midwinter break."

"That's dedication, and one reason why you're such a terrific teacher. It's understandable that Max would pull back at a time like this. I'm sure that once Ava gets well, he'll come around."

"I doubt that." Not according to their recent conversations.

Megan had all but shredded her napkin. She tossed it toward the garbage and missed. She was no closer to finding love than she'd been a month ago, at least not the reciprocal kind. "Why do I try so hard to make the man in my life happy when it never works? They all leave."

"Because—" Her mother hesitated. "Do you really want me to answer that?"

"I meant it in a rhetorical sense, but go ahead."

"All right. Losing your father so suddenly was a huge blow to both of us. Sometimes I think it was worse for you as a twelve-year-old girl than for me."

Megan frowned. "You suffered horribly."

"I was devastated. But your dad's heart attack was easier for me to understand."

"Oh, I understood. He died."

"Do you remember the day it happened?"

Every detail. "He invited me to go birding with him and I refused. We had words, then I stomped out of the house and went to Evie's down the street."

"I had papers to grade, so off he went alone. From what the EMTs said, he appeared to be exiting the car at the edge of the woods when he had the heart attack."

"I hate that our last conversation was an angry one." Even after all this time, Megan felt terrible about that. "If I'd just given in and gone with him...."

"It wouldn't have mattered—his heart still would've given out that day. He had a congenital defect no one had detected."

Megan didn't want to think about that. "We're supposed to be discussing my failed relationships. Why are we talking about Dad?"

"You're smart—you'll figure it out."

"Can't you just tell me?" Megan pleaded.

"It'll make more sense if you put it together yourself."

"Spoken like a teacher."

"Takes one to know one."

Her mother gave her a chance to think for a few minutes before she spoke again. "I can almost see the wheels turn in your mind. What are you coming up with?"

"I've always believed that if I'd been nicer, Dad wouldn't have died that day, but it's not true." The pieces began to fall into place and at last, they made sense. "I've been applying the same faulty logic to my romantic relationships," Megan mused with amazement. "Thinking that if I'm agreeable and work extra hard to please the man in my life, he'll stick around. That's not true, either."

She smacked her forehead with the heel of her hand. "Why has it taken till today for me to get that?"

Her mother smiled. "The important thing is, you figured it out." She checked her watch. "I should get home to Bennett. He's waiting patiently for his scone, which I left in the car."

At the door Megan gave her a grateful hug. "Thanks, Mom. I love you."

"You're welcome. Love you, too."

As Megan showered and dressed she reflected on this morning's revelations.

Understanding the motives behind her behavior changed how she viewed herself. Which was all well and good, but how was she going to use her newfound insights?

How would she use her new insights to change? Megan was still mulling that over while she rocked an infant girl Saturday afternoon.

"You don't care about pleasing me or anyone else—you only want your needs met," she cooed to the fidgeting bundle in her arms. "What a smart girl you are. I can learn a thing or two from you."

And miracle—the little one calmed down and took more than four ounces of formula. Quite a feat for a six-pound newborn.

Megan marveled over the lesson this tiny baby had taught her. And came to a momentous decision.

No more putting a man's wants and needs ahead of her own. From this moment on, she'd please herself first.

21

Megan celebrated the first day of midwinter break shopping the Presidents' Day sales with Ingrid. The mall they chose was packed.

"I want to buy new lingerie," Ingrid said as they made their way to the entrance. "A girl can't have too many sexy underthings. Guys appreciate it."

Unless they were in a big hurry. Like Max the night they'd made love. He'd been too busy getting rid of her bra and panties to pay attention to them.

But Megan wasn't thinking about him anymore.

"Let's start at that cute shoe place at the far end of the mall and stop at the lingerie shop on the way back to the entrance," she said.

"Fine with me," Ingrid said. "I could use a new pair of shoes. I'm thinking boots, something sexy for Logan." She threw Megan a contrite look. "Should I avoid talking about my new guy?"

"Not at all. I'm happy one of us found love."

"We're not quite there yet—neither of us has used the L word—but it's just a matter of time." Ingrid beamed.

"All right, I lied," Megan confessed as they entered the shoe store. "I'm super jealous."

A display of pastel ankle boots caught her eye. "Such pretty spring colors, and twenty percent off today only. A deal we can't pass up."

She and Ingrid grinned at each other and began a serious study of the styles.

"Check out these taupe babies with the three-inch heels," Ingrid gushed. "I can't live without them."

"That's me, with the pale aqua lace-ups. We have to try them on."

They signaled a clerk, sat down, and went to work.

Moments later Ingrid modeled her boots and whistled at Megan. "Those aquas look good on you. Wear them with a short skirt and every guy with eyes will sit up and take notice."

Megan laughed. "I wouldn't mind that, but I'm buying them for me." She lowered her voice. "That's why I'm wearing my best satin lace bra and panties under this pullover and jeans—just for me."

Her friend gave her a sideways look. "You

don't usually do stuff like that. What's gotten into you?"

"Why should I save my pretty underwear for a man, when wearing it for myself makes me feel special? And another thing—I am who I am, warts and all. Take it or leave it, guys, because from now on, I'm all about pleasing myself."

Stating her decision out loud for the first time felt great.

"I like that," Ingrid said. "Look out, world. Does this mean you're already over Max?" she asked as they paid for the shoes and left.

Not even close. "No, but I'm not going to sit around moping and feeling sorry for myself. I have a life to live."

"All right! Have you re-upped your online dating contract?"

Megan shook her head. "Never again. I hate meeting guys that way."

"But if you want marriage and a baby..."

"That's the dream, but as you, my mom, and Bennett remind me from time to time, I don't need a man to be a mother. I'm going to apply for single-parent adoption."

Her friend gaped at her. "But you always say you want a partner to help raise your child."

"I do, but I can manage on my own. Here's why." Megan ticked off the reasons on her fingers. "My townhouse has two bedrooms, I have plenty of money in my savings account, a good job with summers off, and a mother and stepfather eager to welcome a grandchild with open arms. I'll be fine."

"I believe you. Where to next?"

"I could use a new pair of jeans," Megan said.

Ingrid pointed across the mall. "Over there. I'm curious. If—or should I say when— you run into Max, what will you say? Because you seem to keep turning up at the same place at the same time."

Over the weekend Megan had given that some thought. "I'll remind myself that it's his choice not to be with me, and his loss. Then I'll wish him well and mean it."

"I like your new attitude! I have to say that if it was me in that situation, I'd feel sad."

"It'll almost kill me. After all, I am in love with the man. But he'll never know. Check this out." Megan showed off the big, fake smile she'd practiced in front of the bathroom mirror.

"Very convincing. Here's the jeans store, and look at those cute styles in the window." Ingrid rubbed her hands together in anticipation.

"When we're done there, let's stop at the candy shop and pick up a few treats for Ava," Megan said.

Several hours later the backseat of Ingrid's car was piled with purchases. Megan sank into the passenger seat. "That was fun."

"We found some real bargains." They chatted about this and that before Ingrid asked, "Are you excited to see Ava tomorrow?"

Megan nodded. "I have lots of goodies for her —the candy I bought, homemade cookies, the stuffed puppy we all chipped in to buy, a card from her classmates, and some homework."

"She's going to love it all—especially seeing you." Ingrid pulled up to the townhouse. "Are you spending the night in Portland?"

"No. Max is coming up Wednesday and I'd rather not see him. Besides, I need one day to clean house and prep for school Thursday."

"Have fun up there, and tell Ava we're all pulling for her."

"I will."

~

"MISS SPENSER IS COMING TOMORROW!" Ava exclaimed when Max phoned her Monday evening.

As relieved as he was to hear the excitement in her little voice, he didn't want to talk about Megan. Not with anyone, even his niece. Too much of a downer. He needed to forget about her and move on.

She needed to forget him, too.

"What did you do today?" he asked.

"I watched a movie. Tonight I got chocolate pudding for dessert."

Her first mention of food in a long time. Max grinned. "Chocolate pudding, huh? Lucky you.

That medicine you're talking must be working—you sound better than you have in weeks."

"I don't like it. It tastes yucky and makes my tummy hurt and my bones ache."

Poor kid. "The nurses and your mom know that, right?"

"Uh-huh. They're trying to fix it." She yawned. "I'm tired, Uncle Max. I'm ready to go sleep. Do you want to talk to Mama?"

"Nah. Tell her I'll call tomorrow night unless I'm busy with an emergency."

" 'Kay." Another yawn.

"Sleep good and tight," he said, his usual bedtime sendoff.

"With all my might."

22

Both Max and Helen had warned Megan that Ava needed a great deal of rest. For that reason, when she arrived at the hospital she texted Helen. I'm here. Is Ava up for company?

She heard back immediately. Come on up!

Clutching the card and bag full of gifts, Megan entered the elevator. As eager as she was to see Ava she was also nervous. Rocking crack babies was one thing. Visiting a critically ill student was a whole different experience.

No matter. She'd apply the same principles that stood her well whether she cared for the babies or worked in the classroom—be supportive and treat everyone with love and respect.

The crowded elevator stopped on every level until it finally reached the right floor. As Megan headed down the hall toward Ava's room she glimpsed children of different ages sitting or lying in brightly colored rooms, no doubt decorated to brighten young spirits.

Ava's door was open. Before going in, Megan paused unseen and observed the situation. Ava lay propped up in bed, with Helen and four adults about the ages of Megan's mom and Bennett in chairs on either side. There was one empty chair, probably for her.

One of the men, graying and handsome, looked like an older version of Max. Megan's heart hitched with longing and hurt. She wanted to turn around and bolt.

Did any of them know about her and Max? Wait—who cared if they did? Today's visit had nothing to do with Max. She was here for Ava.

Here goes. Forcing a smile, she knocked to announce herself and entered the room.

Ava's face lit up. "Miss Spenser!"

Megan knew the girl had lost a lot of weight, but wasn't prepared for the gaunt cheeks and pale, almost translucent skin. She managed to stifle her alarm. "Gosh, it's good to see you, Ava."

After setting her things on the empty chair, she gave her student a gentle but heartfelt hug. When she straightened, Helen beamed at her.

Both men rose to their feet. She extended her arm. "I'm Megan Spenser."

"Brian Meier," Max's father replied, his handshake firm. "This is my wife, Nora. We're Ava's grandparents. We've heard good things about you."

"We're also her grandparents—Gwen and Alan Chernick," said a pretty woman with eyes the same whiskey-brown color as Max's. No doubt, his mother. She nodded at Megan's new ankle boots. "What a luscious color."

"Thanks. I just got them."

Although Max's divorced parents didn't so much as glance at each other, they seemed civil enough.

Megan retrieved the card and bag of gifts and brought them to Ava. "These are for you. First, this card from your classmates. Everyone at school misses you."

The large card, decorated with messages, yarn, glitter, and drawings, was big enough to fill Ava's lap.

An enormous smile lit her face. "Look what I got, Mama!"

Helen wiped a tear away. "It's truly special."

"I'll pass that on," Megan said.

After several long minutes of reading the well wishes and enjoying the drawings, Ava lost interest. Helen propped the card in the windowsill. "From here you'll be able to see it all the time."

Next, Megan handed over the bag. Ava pulled out the tin of cookies Megan had baked, the candy from the mall, and the stuffed puppy from the faculty and staff. She hugged the puppy.

"Your mom told me your favorite cookies are lemon bars," Megan said. "That's what's in the tin. Shall I open it for you?"

Ava glanced at Helen. "Is it okay, Mama?"

"I don't see why not."

After selecting a small bar, Ava took a tentative bite. "Yummy." She managed to eat almost half of it before she set it down.

"Those look delicious," Helen said. "Ava, would you mind sharing them with me, your grandparents, and Megan?"

Ava shook her head. Megan declined, and while the family enjoyed the treats, she slid a folder from her purse. "I also brought homework, so you can keep up with the rest of the class."

"I like homework," Ava said, but it was obvious she was exhausted.

Helen smoothed her daughter's hair back. "We'll do our best, Miss Spenser."

"Go at your own pace, Ava. Helen, feel free to contact me anytime with questions. There's a self-addressed, stamped envelope in the folder. When Ava finishes her work, mail it to me. I'll grade and send it back with a new assignment."

Ava's eyelids began to droop.

"She needs rest," Helen said.

"Of course. Thanks for letting me visit, Ava. I'll let your classmates, Principal Herman, and everyone at school know how you're doing. Get well soon, all right?"

"I will."

"Come back again," Max's father said.

Helen shook her head. "You know what a long drive it is, Dad. I'll walk you out, Megan."

As soon as they stepped out of the room, Helen shut the door. "You have no idea how much your visit meant to Ava—to all of us," she said on the way to the elevator.

Touched, Megan smiled. "It meant a lot to me, too. Have the doctors said when she can come home?"

"Hopefully by the end of the week. Then she'll need to spend another few weeks recuperating at home."

Such a long convalescence. "When you're back in Guff's Lake, I'll come visit again."

"That'd be great. Has Max been in touch?"

Megan's smile slipped. "Mostly to update me on Ava's progress."

"That's what I was afraid of," Helen muttered. "I really like you, Megan, and I'd so hoped you and he were still seeing each other."

As did Megan, but she was determined to put the whole thing behind her. "He told you about that?"

"Not in so many words, but when he drove Ava and me to Portland that awful night, he mentioned you. I could tell he liked you." Helen shook her head. "I'm sorry it didn't work out."

Megan didn't want to think about that. She wanted to move on. "You don't have to worry about me. I'm doing all right."

More or less. As long as she stuck to pleasing herself.

"If it's any consolation, I think my brother is an idiot."

"It helps."

At the elevator, the two women hugged. "Have a safe trip home," Helen said. "You'll hear from me soon."

FEBRUARY WAS Max's month to serve as a paramedic. Monday was busy but Tuesday was crazy, with one call after another. It was close to midnight when he returned from a trip to the cardiac unit at Rogue Valley General Hospital. Man, he was beat—or would be once the adrenaline coursing through him wore off. That happened while he helped ready the aid car for the next emergency.

When he finished, he plodded to his room to snag some zz's while he could. On the way, he checked his cell phone. Even when he wasn't able to call Helen or wish Ava a good night's rest, his sister sent photos and a newsy text or voice mail. Tonight, nada. Nothing from his parents, either.

What was up with that?

Megan had been in Portland today and he wanted an update. At this hour it was too late to check in with his family but she could still be awake. Heck, this was midwinter break and she didn't have to get up in the morning. They weren't seeing each other anymore but they still touched base about his niece.

Max sent a text. How did it go with Ava?

He didn't hear back. She was probably asleep —or on a date with some guy. The thought dampened his already low spirits.

Ending a relationship had never hurt this bad.

As tired as he was, falling asleep took awhile. Between tossing and turning and a second emergency call, he started Wednesday seriously sleep deprived.

He was on the way to the apparatus bay to clock out when Megan texted a reply. Visit with Ava good. Pls no more texts or calls.

What the hell? Max stumbled and almost lost his balance.

Downstairs, the rest of the crew had clocked out and a fair number were about to head to Rosemary's for breakfast.

"You look like shit," Tony greeted him. "Why don't you join us at Rosemary's before you leave for Portland?"

"You're no prize, either," Max snarled. "No time for breakfast. I need to get up there."

"Yeah, well you need coffee more."

"I'll get some on the road."

"Up to you. Be safe."

Some twenty miles out of town, in serious need of both caffeine and food, Max stopped at a

Golden Arches. Before he pulled back onto the freeway, he phoned Megan. Her text this morning rankled, and he wanted an explanation.

"Did you not read my text?" she said, without even a standard hello.

"Hi to you, too. What's with that, anyway? Are you seeing someone who doesn't want you texting me?"

"No one tells me who I can and can't text." She sounded huffy. "And FYI, I'm not dating anyone. I've stopped looking."

Max couldn't believe his ears. Confused, he scratched the back of his neck. "What about getting married and starting a family?"

"Who says I need to marry in order to have a baby? I've decided to adopt instead. It's better to raise a child with two parents, but I'll be a good mother regardless."

She was full of surprises today. "No kidding."

"I'm sensing your disapproval," she said. "But I approve. That's what matters."

She sounded...different. Sure of herself in a way Max admired.

"I don't disapprove at all. About the text you sent. You expect updates from me about Ava, but when I want the same from you, you tell me not to contact you anymore?"

"It's not a good idea for me to hear from you when I need to move on. From now on, Helen will be my contact."

In other words, Get out of my life.

And he thought he felt rotten before. "Uh, okay."

"Be happy, Max."

And she was gone.

23

"That went well, even if talking to Max nearly did me in," Megan told Bling after Max's call. "No worries—I'll get over him." Sooner rather than later. "Got that, heart?"

The old Megan would have indulged in another pity party, but those days were behind her. Determined to keep her mind off Max she cleaned house, then prepped for tomorrow's school day. When she finished that, she reached for her purse and coat.

Bling meowed. "You want to know where I'm going? To the grocery. I'm in the mood to bake something decadent, but I'm missing a few key ingredients." Chocolate chips, shredded coconut, and whatever else tempted her. "I may as well pick up more art supplies for school, and I'll probably stop at the pet store and get you a new toy because you're such a good boy. Keep an eye on the house while I'm gone."

Seemingly content with her explanation and busy grooming himself, the tom didn't bother to react.

The very act of getting out boosted her spirits. By the time she loaded her groceries into the trunk of her car, she was almost smiling.

MAX ARRIVED in Portland running on empty and in a foul temper. In no shape to see his family or his niece right now, he texted that he'd arrived but needed to sleep for a while.

After inhaling a sandwich and chips from a convenience store, he locked himself in his motel room and crashed. Several hours later he woke up in a better mood, but not by much. The hollow feeling inside was tough to ignore.

Still not up to facing his family, and needing to clear the last dregs of sleep from his head, he wandered into Buster's Café for a double shot of caffeine.

As usual at mid-afternoon business was slow and most of the tables empty. Seated at his regular table, Jasper bent over a paperback, a plate of cookies, coffee, and his checkerboard within reach.

When Max pivoted from the counter with a steaming mug, the older man glanced up. "Hey, buddy, how're you doing?" he called out.

"Not bad." A total lie, but Max wasn't about to

air his dirty laundry to anyone, let alone a guy he barely knew.

Jasper set his book aside and nodded at the empty chair across from him. "Care for a game of checkers?"

Max started to shake his head, then changed his mind. What the hell. He sat down.

"You never told me your name," Jasper said.

"Max."

"I like that—it means 'the greatest.' Jasper means 'jewel.' "

"You're a trivia buff."

"Only with names. I find it interesting that folks seem to fit their given names."

Max almost laughed at that. He was as far from "the greatest" as a man could be.

"I bought too many biscotti," his tablemate said as he set out the checkers. "Help yourself."

Max polished off a couple of the treats. "You weren't kidding when you said you're here all the time."

"I've been a regular since the place opened some thirty years ago. When I worked at the hospital I came here to get away from the job."

"You worked at the hospital?" Max was surprised. "I pictured you as more the forestry type."

"It's the hair and beard. After I retired I let both grow. Before that, I was a clean-cut, pediatric social worker. Sick kids often need a neutral adult to talk to. Same with their families."

Max had never thought about that, but it

made sense. Professionals in Jasper's line of work didn't judge or criticize like Helen and his crewmates did.

"Anyway, after I retired, this became my office of sorts. Then when my wife died... I like the ambiance here. The coffee and bakery items are decent, and I've met a fair share of good people."

"Sorry about your wife."

"Thanks. How's that niece of yours?"

"Improving. We hope she'll be able to come home soon."

"You can't beat that for good news. You don't seem happy, though." Jasper moved his checkers piece to the last row of Max's side of the board. "King me."

Already? Max crowned the piece. "You're a wily player. I'd better pay more attention."

Jasper chuckled, then raised his eyebrows in an "I'm listening, tell me more" pose.

Screw that. Max moved his piece forward. "There's this woman..." he heard himself say.

"Ah." Jasper made a countermove.

His comfortable silence and the fact that Max didn't really know him changed his mind about talking. He shrugged. "Long story short, I broke up with her. Now I'm rethinking that."

Seriously? He hadn't consciously considered reversing himself, but hearing the words from his own lips... Yep, he was doing exactly that.

"You're feeling down because she doesn't want to try again."

"She doesn't know—I haven't told her."

"You should."

"It's not that simple." Megan didn't want to talk to him anymore. She wanted to move on. Max advanced a checker.

"You a bank robber or a murderer?"

"Hell, no. I'm a firefighter down in Guff's Lake."

"You really are among the greatest, a real-life hero."

Max dipped his head. "I do my best."

"You live in a nice town, too."

"You've been there?"

"Summers back in the day, my wife and I liked to set up camp and hike and fish in the Siskiyous. We always ended the trip with a stay at the resort hotel there. Beautiful country."

"I live near the resort and enjoy the lake and foothills whenever I can."

"Lucky you. About this woman... Why did you break up with her?"

Max stuck with his pat answer. "I've never been a fan of long-term commitments. Short and sweet works best for me."

Eyes narrowed in thought, Jasper stroked his beard. "What are you afraid of?"

"What kind of question is that?" Max growled. "Nothing scares me."

Except his own feelings. He wasn't going to admit that.

Unruffled, Jasper calmly regarded him.

"Everyone is afraid of something. Take me. The thought of flying gives me hives. I avoid planes whenever possible, and I've been known to take a two-day bus trip to avoid a six-hour flight."

"I'm onto your tricks. You shared, now you expect me to."

Jasper grinned. "Caught me. You're a smart one. How about answering the question."

"Why should I tell you anything?"

"Don't unless you want to, but I happen to care. I'm wired that way."

Under his level gaze, Max shifted in his seat. "I've lived through my share of loss. The death of my younger sister, my parents' divorce... Who needs it?"

Jasper rocked back in his chair. "You leave before you get left."

Max had never looked at it that way.

His seatmate wasn't finished. "As a firefighter you put your life on the line all the time to save others. That takes selflessness and mental courage."

Max nodded. "Without those I couldn't do my job."

"Emotional risks are another thing altogether. You avoid them."

Talk about hitting the bull's-eye. "Well, yeah. I'd have to be crazy not to."

Another direct look. "Love has its ups and downs. Still, I'd choose it anytime over loneliness." Jasper double-jumped and neatly captured two of Max's checkers. "But that's me. Only you can decide whether you want a lifetime of short relationships and little emotional risk, or something more meaningful."

Pretending to study the board, Max kicked that around.

"My friend, you have a lot to think about."

He had that right. Right then, Max received a text from Helen. "That's my sister—my niece's mom." He read the message.

Ava's blood tests look good. Going home Saturday!

Max grinned. "Great news—we're taking my niece home this weekend. I need to get to the hospital. Thanks for the game and biscotti."

"I enjoyed talking with you, too." Jasper smiled back. "Take good care of that little girl, and best of luck with your woman."

24

With Ava home and improving by the day, Max had time to catch up on woodworking projects. Over the next two weeks he designed and started the coffee table his customer had commissioned, crafted his niece's jewelry box, and made major inroads on the headboard for Adam and Sam.

He also continued to chew on Jasper's observations. The man sure knew his stuff. Within minutes he'd pinpointed Max's fears and the reason he stuck with short-term relationships—to protect himself. Better to leave before there was a chance of falling in love and getting hurt.

He got that, but it didn't change anything. He was still scared and still floundering over what to do about Megan.

In his workshop early one Thursday morning, he decided to sand the rough edges of the headboard, then size and cut maple slabs for the coffee table. He'd barely begun before he received a call from the community college. They wanted to set up an interview about the fire safety course.

That part of his life had lined up nicely. Pleased, he grinned.

On the radio, Alicia Keys was singing about love. Max smoothed and contoured the headboard and thought about Adam. Despite an initial reluctance to tie himself down with Sam, he was now fully committed to her and her son, whom he planned to adopt. Their future seemed bright.

As of Christmas Eve, Rafe and Jillian were also engaged.

Max envied both of his crewmates. Pretty strange, considering that even the thought of commitment gave him the willies.

Even crazier, for the first time in his adult life he could see himself in a real relationship. The kind that lasted. With Megan.

He shut off the sander before he ruined the headboard and frowned. Since when had he come up with that? Hell if he knew. Anyway, for now, it was a thought, nothing more.

And a feeling. He cared about her more than any woman he'd ever known. Was he man enough to set his fears aside and love her the way she deserved?

It'd happened anyway. He already did.

He loved Megan.

Dumbfounded, he sat down hard. Admitting it felt good—and bad. He was still wary. Hell, he was scared out of his gourd.

All of a sudden he needed air. He stood up again, threw on a down jacket, and left the house. On foot, he headed toward the foothills near Guff's Lake Resort and hiked up.

He saw no other people, which suited him fine. He'd never been inclined to introspection, but now he dug deep. Love hurt. Did he really want to risk getting serious with Megan?

While the question rattled around his head he tromped around for hours, his breath clouded and his hands cold despite warm gloves. In late February, winter was still in full tilt up here, but on careful inspection he noted signs of approaching spring. Patches of melting snow, a pregnant deer, an occasional bird calling out.

Spring—a time of hope and renewal.

Renewal sounded good. Maybe it was time to ditch his old views for a new lease on life and embrace his own fresh start.

Once Max made up his mind, following through was easy. He sucked in a breath, blew it out, and let go of the fear that had weighted him down for far too long.

A subtle tension he'd never realized he carried vanished, and he knew with certainty that he wanted a future with Megan—risks and all.

He couldn't wait to tell her, but first he'd make her a gift that expressed his feelings. What he had in mind needed just the right wood. At last he knew what to do with the slab of walnut that had been sitting in his workshop for months.

Filled with purpose he headed home. He worked all night and most of Friday, but the end product was worth losing sleep over. Megan's gift had turned out well. She was sure to like it—if he wasn't too late.

They hadn't spoken in a month. He'd hurt her and she wanted to move on.

What if she wouldn't give him a second chance?

A whole new fear had him swallowing, but now that he knew what he wanted, he refused to let anything stop him. Buckling into the Explorer, he sped off.

"HEADING over to Helen's to see Ava?" Ingrid asked Friday after school.

Hurrying to tidy the classroom so that she and her friend could walk out together, Megan shook her head. "They're expecting me tomorrow after I leave the hospital. Are you seeing Logan later?"

At the mention of her guy, Ingrid seemed to glow with happiness. "He'll be over in about an hour with wine and a couple of T-bones. We're grilling out and relaxing."

"Sounds perfect." Megan smiled. "I wouldn't be surprised if you moved in together."

"We're talking about it. What's on your agenda tonight?"

"The usual—wine, popcorn, and vegging out in front of the tube. I'm also going to look for more information on the adoption sites." She hadn't selected one yet, but had narrowed down her choices.

"Speaking of TV, Casablanca is showing at eight on the movie classics chann—" Wide-eyed, Ingrid broke off.

Megan glanced over her shoulder to see what had startled her friend.

Max.

He stood in the doorway, big and gorgeous as ever. Her wayward heart sighed with pleasure. They hadn't seen each other or spoken in a month, which made no difference in her feelings for him. She loved him as much as ever. Getting over him was going to take a long time.

"Hey." He nodded, his face unreadable.

"Hi." Uncomfortable, she glanced at the paper bag in his hand, tied at the neck with twine. "What's in there?"

"I'll get to that. Can we talk?" He eyed Ingrid. "Alone."

"Got it." Ingrid started to leave, then hesitated. "Do you want me to stay, Megan?"

"I'm fine."

"You look beautiful," he commented in the sudden silence.

"You don't have to say that. It's been a hectic week and a long day. I know I'm a mess."

"Not to me." His eyes shone with feeling. Almost as if he cared.

Had he been drinking? She sniffed the air but didn't smell alcohol. "Are you feeling all right?"

"Better than I have in a long time."

Confused, she frowned. "You're not making any sense."

Max shut the door. "Sit down and I'll explain."

Curious, Megan sank onto her desk chair while he pulled a folding chair from the closet and set it up beside her.

"I'll get right to the point," he said, placing the mysterious bag on the floor. "About my bad habit of ducking out of a relationship before I get in too deep..."

Oh, please, not that again. "Don't, Max. I'm over it."

His shoulders seemed to sag before he straightened again. "You haven't heard what I came here to say. Let me speak my piece."

"All right."

"I always said love and commitment weren't for me."

"Yes, I remember." How could she forget?

"With us, things got intense fast, so fast, I didn't stop to think about what it meant. Except that I liked you and wanted more. Then Ava got sick and I flipped out. I kept thinking about Janet."

His bleak look mirrored Megan's own sadness and heartache. "I remember that, too. But Ava's okay now."

"Yeah, but at the time we didn't know that. A lot of crap bubbled up and I pulled away from you."

"What kind of crap?"

Instead of answering the question he stood, tossed his jacket aside, paced the room, and in general seemed on edge. Abruptly he sat down again.

"You want to know why I steered away from serious relationships? To protect myself from getting hurt. It was a trust thing—I didn't trust that someone I cared for would stick around. Then you came along. You had me right from the start, but I was too thick-headed to realize it. No, I was scared. Of my feelings, of what would happen if we didn't work out."

He picked up the bag, cleared his throat. "I don't think that way anymore."

While she tried to make sense of that, he thrust the bag at her. "This is for you."

It felt bulky and solid in her hands. "What is it?" she asked, pulling at the twine.

"Something that expresses my feelings better than words."

The tie fell to the ground and the paper bag

with it, revealing a four-inch-square wood box. Lightly stained so that the grain showed through. Simple, yet elegant. "Oh, Max, it's gorgeous." She ran her fingers over the smooth, satiny surface several times. "I've never seen anything like this."

"It's a one of a kind. So are you, Megan, and I can't imagine a future without you."

Words she'd dreamed of her whole life. But. "A month ago I'd have given just about anything to hear you say that. Since then, I've changed. I won't settle for less than I want."

He turned a little green. "You moved on."

"No—I'm still in love with you."

His expression lightened and the color returned to his face. "You mean that?"

She nodded. "But I want to get married and have a baby. Or as I mentioned before, do a single-parent adoption. If you don't want marriage and children, then no matter how much I love you we aren't meant to be together."

"Then we're good. I see our relationship as a marriage and a partnership. I can't wait to make a baby with you. Maybe two."

Megan nearly fell out of her chair. "Are you sure?"

"More than I've ever been about anything. You haven't opened the box."

"It opens? How?"

"Twist the lid. Like this." He mimed what to do with his fingers.

She followed his directions and the top

swiveled away from the bottom, revealing a hidden compartment. "This is ingenious, Max. You put something in here." She lifted out a wood heart, stained red.

"It's a symbol of my heart. You own it now."

She was going to cry. "You've changed, too."

"A hundred-eighty degrees. A friend helped open my eyes. His name is Jasper and he lives in Portland. Sometime soon I'll take you up to meet him. Knowing you love me... I'm very happy. I love you, too."

Forget going to cry. Tears blurred Megan's eyes. "I never, ever expected those words from you. Say them again?"

"I love you, Megan. Now and forever."

He cupped her face in his big, warm hands, tilted her head, and drew her into a long, tender kiss that left her breathless.

"Let's get married right away and start working on that baby," he said when they came up for air.

She laughed. "I need time to plan the wedding. What do you think about late summer, before the new school year starts?"

"Works for me." Max linked his fingers with hers. "Tonight I want you all to myself. Let's go to your place and order in. Tomorrow we'll tell Helen and Ava. When you're ready, you can introduce me to your mom and stepdad. Sound good?"

Megan smiled. "Like the future I've always dreamed of."

THE END

THANK you for letting me share my stories with you!

IF YOU ENJOYED **MR. JUNE,** help others find this book by recommending it to your friends and by writing a review. If you would like to know when my next release is available and other fun stuff, sign up for my newsletter here: www.annroth.net

THERE ARE 12 sexy firefighter books planned for the **Heroes of Rogue Valley: Calendar Guys**

OTHER BOOKS:

Ann Roth Classics:
Father of the Year
A Place to Belong
My Sisters
Another Life

. . .

Visit me at Facebook facebook.com/AnnRothAuthorPage
    Follow me on Twitter @Ann_Roth
    Email me at ann@annroth.net
    Visit my website www.annroth.net

Thanks, and until next time,
    Ann

ALSO BY ANN ROTH

Ann Roth Classics

A Place to Belong

Father of the Year

Another Life

My Sisters

Dunlin Shores

Book 1 Just the Way You Are

Book 2 Wedding Bell Blues

Book 3 Falling for Mr. Wrong

Book 4: A Special Kind of Love

Firefighters

Book 1 Mr. January

Book 2 Mr. February

Book 3 Mr. March

Book 4: Mr. April

Book 5: Mr. May

Book 6: Mr. June

Book 7: Mr. July

Book 8: Mr. August

Book 9: Mr. September

Book 10: Mr. December

Halo Island

Book 1 All I Want for Christmas

Book 2 The Pilot's Woman

Book 3 Ooh, Baby!

Book 4 The One I Love

Miracle Falls

Book 1 Christmas in Miracle Falls

Book 2 Dream a Little Dream

Book 3 It Had to Be You

Book 4: You're the One That I Want

Saddlers Prairie

Book 1 Since I Fell for You

Book 2 I'll Be There

Book 3 Until There Was You